Hopelessly Devoted to You

Samantha D. Long

Published by Satin Romance
An Imprint of Melange Books, LLC
White Bear Lake, MN 55110
www.satinromance.com

Published in the United States of America.

Cover Design by Ashley Redbird Designs

For my enormous family.
A group full of critiques with hearts full of love!

part one

one

INTRODUCTIONS

His name was as unique as the gorgeous young man who owned it. Texas Conrad the Fourth. He introduced himself as "*Tex*" to which I, who had been lounging in the sun on the beach, looked up and said so smoothly...

"Huh?"

He smiled. The corner of his mouth tugged up just a little more than the other side. "I'm sorry," he said. "I don't mean to bother you, but I'm new around here and I thought I'd introduce myself to people and try to get settled in."

When he had finished talking, his mouth remained open in an awkward friendly smile. I just continued to stare with one hand perched on my forehead above my sunglasses, attempting to dim the bright sun even more. As he stood there, fidgeting and being awkward, I took a moment to give him a once-over. He was built strong and tan. His body was perfect with not necessarily severely cut abs, but the outlined muscles were there. His face had a chiseled look to it. The kind of face you would suspect was the model for all those Greek statues in Rome. The wind blew a wave of sandy blond hair off his forehead.

"So anyway," he said, "my name is Tex."

"Tex?"

"Yeah," he answered brightly. "It's Texas Conrad the Fourth, something or other," he mumbled, "but Tex is what I answer to."

"Family name?"

"Yup."

I stood up brushing sand off myself and held out my hand to him.

"Selena," I told him.

He took my hand gently, repeating my name back to me as he did.

"Not a family name," I added, shaking his hand. "Just me, Selena Marie Ayers."

We were still holding hands. I suddenly felt as if he was taking his time to peruse me and did a mental thank you to Amber for making me wear the black two-piece instead of the comfy one-piece I had originally planned to wear today. She had said that since it was finally tanning weather around here, I had to wear it. The two-piece was a little bit of a tight fit, but it curved with me and even gave the girls a little push upwards. I cocked my head slightly, letting my dark blond hair sweep across my shoulder, and smiled.

"How many people have you met so far?" I asked.

"Just you, Selena."

"Just me? Exactly how long have you been here?"

"All day." He shrugged, smiling again.

"You've been out here all day, and I'm the first person you've seen?"

He licked his lips and one eye squinted in the sun. He looked down for just a moment, then back up. The squint returned with a smile. "Nah," he said, "you aren't the first person I've seen. Just the only one I wanted to meet."

My breath hitched. Now, I ask you. What sixteen-year-old girl wouldn't have fallen in love?

I invited him to sit with me on our overly large beach blanket under the huge rainbow-colored umbrella the boys had rigged into the sand. Those sand anchors are great, but trying to explain to two Neanderthal teenage boys how to use what should be self-explanatory is no picnic. After getting comfortable, I offered him a beverage from our cooler. That click and crisp sound of opening sodas echoed before we each took our first sips.

"So, when did you arrive in Saint Caine, if you're alright with me asking?" I said, taking another sip from my can.

"It's been a few weeks," he answered, turning so the sun was on his back. The effect of the lighting behind that gorgeous tan and smile made him almost angelic. Goodness, I needed to get it together. "But enough about me," he blurted out, reaching out a finger to tap my knee. "I want to know all about you."

I laughed. "You act like we've been discussing you for hours."

"Well," he shrugged, "anything about me is boring."

"I could say the same about myself."

"I seriously doubt that," he said, and the laughing smile faded into a soft, sincere one. Heat crept up my neck and into my cheeks. I bowed my head a little with the blush. After a beat, he scooted closer and said, "Tell me everything. I want to know about your parents, school, everything."

"Alright," I giggled. "Well, we've lived here my whole life, and my parents are the absolute best but don't ever tell them I said that. They would get astronomically big heads about it." I laughed again. "My dad is the neighborhood postman and has been for so long that practically everyone knows him by name. There isn't a store we go into that someone doesn't stop him and start chatting." Tex smiled as nervous laughter bubbled out of me. I scrunch my face while trying to think of what to tell him next. "Um, mom is a retired school teacher, and before you ask about her age, no, she isn't old." I rolled my eyes for emphasis because I get that question a lot. "She taught for twenty years, but when Dad was given the full-time route, she decided to retire early and just be a stay-at-home mom who makes designer dollhouses that she sells for a small fortune."

"She makes dollhouses?" he asked, "Like those open Barbie dream-house things I've seen in commercials?"

"Yes and no. These are more like elaborate ones with carpet and lighting; everything is all handcrafted and painted. She sells them online, too. People have even bought them from overseas."

"Wow! That's impressive. Did she make you one?"

"Only the biggest one ever." I admitted, "Now, let's see... We live over on Maple; um, school is, I don't know... typical, I guess. I mean, if you've seen any movie with a depiction of high school in it, then you pretty much have the gist of any public high school."

"This will be my first public school appearance," Tex said, pulling up his knees and wrapping his forearms around them. I'm pretty sure my mouth dropped.

"Seriously?"

"Yes. My educational journey has consisted of only a very prestigious private school in Dallas."

"Wow," I mouthed, my eyes widening. "You are in for a shock!"

I had never met anyone who hadn't at least experienced a year or so of public school. I couldn't imagine how Tex was going to adapt to such a primal place compared to the structure of a private school. I mean, the kids at our school were practically feral at times. I informed him of this and enjoyed the sound of his laughter. Truthfully, I used to snort when I would hear girls say things like, *"I could just look at him forever"*, all whimsical and swooning, but after meeting this guy, well, I guess you could lump me in with them.

two

A GIRL LIKE ME

You see, I'd never been the girl who always had a boyfriend. That was my besties, Amber and Cass. My life consisted of being the only child of two nerdy but wonderful parents who raised me to know the value of myself. I have always been perfectly happy in my own element. There could be people around and there could not; either way, I was good.

My parents were high school sweethearts who had lived their lives being happy to be with one another. That must be where I get it from. So, as the years went by and middle school brought forth teenage angst, my friends suddenly dissolved into giggling fits over boys we'd known since kindergarten. I did not. Odds are that you're thinking this whole romance on the beach is overdone, and I can't blame you for thinking that. I have rolled my eyes at many romantic movies while my friends gushed and carried on over Ryan Gosling or some other hottie while pretending they were the female lead. Regardless of the cliché, that is exactly what happened on the beach that day, and I'll willingly take the label of sappy romantic teen on this one.

When I arrived back home, my awesome parents, Garrett and Naomi Ayers, were both in the kitchen, giggling like teenagers while cooking dinner. I love that my parents are also best friends. I'm not saying they are perfect by any means, but I know what some home lives are like for a lot of the kids at school, and I've been raised well enough to appreciate the wonderful blessings I've been given.

"Hey, Sel," my dad said, looking back over his shoulder as I came into the kitchen. "We're having steak and garlic-mashed potatoes tonight."

"Yum!" I said, then wiggled my way between them while offering to help. My mom's curly brown hair was pulled up in a loose bun. She is so beautiful, and when she pulls her hair up like this, it accentuates her face and makes her big brown eyes look even bigger. She notices me looking at her with a goofy grin. With a wink of her eye, she elbows me before setting to work on whipping the potatoes.

"What is it?" she asked, scrunching her nose at the splash of potato that launched its way to her cheek. Dad starts humming some tune that sounds like it is from the fifties as he carries the steaks out the back door, heading for the grill.

"Nothing," I said with a shrug. "I was thinking about what a lucky, happy girl I am."

"Really?" she says quizzically, "and what brought on this revelation?"

I almost broke out into a fit of giggles when I thought back to my meeting with Tex on the beach. Heat radiated from my neck to my ears, and I knew my cheeks were red with a blush. Mom knocked a towel over her shoulder, turned to rest her hip against the counter, and tilted her head.

"Selena," she said, "what's with the rosy cheeks?" But before I could answer, her eyes widened, and she sucked in a breath with a knowing look on her face. "You met a boy!" she exclaimed.

I didn't dare acknowledge her with a comment. The heat that had radiated enough to color my cheeks intensified, and I knew I wouldn't be able to get through an interrogation without collapsing into fits of giggles. So, I just squeaked and ran out of the kitchen, heading for the stairs that would take me up to my room. I heard Mom's voice following quickly behind me as I did.

"You don't get off that easy, young lady," she said with a laugh. "I expect details later this evening."

Still giddy with thoughts of the boy on the beach I rushed into my room and collapsed on my fluffy queen-sized bed. My many stuffed pigs flopped and rolled toward me. No one would have ever dreamed this would happen to me. If you knew me at all, you would have said, "That girl there, the one with her face in a book who is hardly wearing any make-up and wearing the most mundane of outfits—T-shirt and jeans—will graduate at the top of her class and go to some uptight school. Eventually, she will graduate with a degree in some type of English study, like creative writing or journalism or something, and end up marrying one of the equally ordinary guys from one of her classes." No one would have said that there would be a gorgeous guy approaching her while she sunbathed who would completely sweep her off her feet and send her heart pounding against her chest and back at the same time. I rolled over and rested my head on the crook of my elbow, thinking about all that had happened from the first moment I heard his velvety voice.

three

Not long after our introductions on the beach, my two friends and their boyfriends had come up from the water. Amber and Cassey have been my best friends since grade school. Amber, who is barely over five feet, and her six-foot-tall boyfriend Pete Myers have been a thing since freshman year. Cassey, our tall and unfairly built, shining blond bombshell, has been off and on with Derek Cooper since middle school. Cassey is a full-on witch with a *B* and does not care who knows it. Aside from that, she is fiercely loyal, and we love her. She and Derek will most definitely get married someday. And eventually, someday after that, they will most likely get divorced.

I still don't understand how the three of us just happened to click on that day in third grade, but every time I think about it, I can't help but laugh and grin. It was raining that day, so outside recess was canceled. All the classes had to eat lunch and play in their rooms. After pizza and milk, I wandered over to where the puzzles and board games were. I pulled out the *Chutes and Ladders* game just as Cassey reached for it. I pulled it back my way as she pulled it to herself. It most likely would have ended in a screaming fight over who was going to get the game, but that was the exact moment when Amber came up to us, standing right in between us, looking down at the game. She shoved her glasses up her nose and smiled at Cassey, and then me as she said, "This will be fun, you guys; let's play."

We spent the entire recess playing the game and sharing the snacks our teacher passed out to assist in keeping us quiet. From that day forward, we were inseparable at school. Middle school is where Derek and Pete suddenly went from gross boys that could not be in our club to the girls batting their eyelashes and laughing at jokes that weren't the least bit funny. At first, they were just annoying brats who refused to leave us alone, but as time went on, they eventually worked their way into Amber and Cass's hearts. Even though I've always been the fifth wheel, they never once made me feel like I was ever unwelcome when we all hung out together. I guess that's why I was so excited for them to meet Tex that day. It was like I was saying, *Look guys, I'm not going to be an imposition anymore!*

I introduced them all to Tex and endured quite a lot of elbow jabs and sneaky looks thereafter. We invited Tex to Cassey's house for our nightly bonfire, and by the time he needed to leave, we were already at the hand-holding stage.

I learned so much about him in just those few hours that I have kept them with me as if they were the most important things I could ever know. Texas Conrad the Fourth moved to Saint Caine because his family is in the oil and gas business. His father hopes to develop ground in our little town. Just two blocks past the Dairy Barn, down from the most popular beach strip off Mason Street, he is building one of two Texacon stations. They are gas and general stores named after the men in his family, all the Texas Conrads from his great-grandfather, who first ventured the family into business when he struck oil while attempting to dig a new well, and on down the line. The first Texacon station went up in Corpus Christi, Texas, and as of today, there are over thirty of them between Texas, Louisiana, Kansas, and New Mexico. Most stations are in small city areas, but Tex says it's his dad's dream to have Texacon make a big name in Dallas.

The second station is being built in the heart of Saint Caine, where all the businesses are up and down a forever-busy interstate. The area is busy with outlet malls, mini golf, food venues, and lots of entertainment traps. It's a tourist's paradise.

"My father plans to swell the bank on these deals," Tex told us as we all gathered around the fire in the chill of the summer night.

He had my hand in his and gave it a little squeeze. In that moment, I finally got to feel what I had been envious of. Please don't misunderstand me. I truly am and have always been very happy for my friends. It's just… Well, I'm sure at some point in your life you can relate to having been the third wheel, right? In my situation, though, I was always the fifth wheel. The boys we grew up with and the few I've dated here and there were fine and all, but I've never felt those feelings, you know. The ones I'm feeling now. So I'll admit, I was a little jealous of what my friends had. Maybe now I can take part instead of spectating, and you know what? The best thing about these businesses going up here is that Tex would be planting roots. This was not going to be just a summer romance for me. He was going to be enrolling in Saint C. High as a junior, just like me. We were both between the ages of sixteen and twenty-one. We met on a beautiful beach on a day when I hadn't even wanted to go and was made to wear my best two-piece suit. The best part of it all, according to Tex, was that he had a weakness for big brown eyes. His soft voice was barely a whisper as he slid the sunglasses from my face and said those very words. Now how did he know the color of my eyes when I had those glasses on the whole time?

Saint C. High isn't really any different from any other high school in the country. You drive down the interstate, get off on Country Road 60 (which is an overpass), take a left at the stop sign, and carry on until you see the huge black iron gates beside the stone monolith announcing you have reached Saint C. High and Middle Schools. We have to trek up a hill to get to the parking lots located at the front and back of the combined school. The middle school takes up the right side of the building, and the high school houses the left. It's around ten years old, so it's still nice on the inside, but it wouldn't hurt the administration to choke up on the janitors a bit.

Our colors are dark navy blue and vibrant gold, the same as W.V.U. The rumor is that the first superintendent of our school district was an alum, but that's neither here nor there. Cass, Amber, and I exited my car and clicked our shoes the entire way up the concrete stairs and through the front doors of the building. We always have to start in the gym on the first day of school, so we strolled our way down the "*Soldier Pride*" hall, up another flight of steps, and down the top floor hall before turning into the enormous two-level gymnasium. It's close to an hour before the freshmen are sorted out and the rest of us are let loose. We all know that not a whole lot is going to be happening today, so just about everyone is taking their sweet time getting to class and gossiping about anything and everything on their way.

As expected, the students were all buzzed with the news

about a new student who was a good-looking rich boy with an oil tycoon for a father. The expected mean girl entourage, also known as the "*school ho patrol*" had set to work from the first bell. Patricia Kearns and her bulimic entourage made their way to Tex the minute he stepped into the office for his schedule. Patty slid up beside him, slinging her dark black hair over her shoulder, and leaned against the counter which, in turn, pushed her breasts practically out of her blouse. She pretended to need something from Miss Varn, but in reality, she just wanted an excuse to get Tex's attention. I'm not going to lie here. He's a flesh-and-blood guy, so his eyes saw the boobs, and then he looked away. Patty cleared her throat and tapped his shoulder.

"New in town?" she asked him, fluttering her false eyelashes.

I'll give this to Patty; we may not like the trick at all, but we'll acknowledge that she has great make-up skills and is built attractively. Our dislike comes from the fact that she knows this and gladly uses these attributes to get her way, and the boys, regularly. Tex gave her a friendly smile. He's a good guy like that.

"Yes, ma'am," he said, "it's my first day to be a soldier."

"Oh," she giggled, "lucky you and lucky us. Our Saint C. soldiers could use a little more muscle on the battlefield." She squeezed his arm. "Do you play?"

"I do, but I haven't made the team yet." He said to her while pulling his backpack up on one shoulder and looking at his schedule. "I'd better find my locker and these classes." He told her, moving past her minions and getting undressed with six eyes in the process.

"Yummy," was the comment straight out of the mouth of Tabitha Trumane, who emphasized the comment by licking the red lips that matched her flaming red hair.

"Indeed." Patty agreed, giving Tabitha a dirty look. "Keep your tits in your shirt, Tabs; I saw him first."

Tabitha was giving Patty an equally evil look and was just about to let her have it when their ever-present lackey piped up.

"Um, sorry to stop the cat fight," Jadynn Woods told them, making her voice sound babyish as if she did feel sorry for them, "but I don't think you saw him first after all."

All eyes, at that moment, followed Jadynn's pointed finger and looked out the office glass to witness Tex wrapping his arms around my waist and spinning me in the air before setting me down. I turned quickly and, seeing it was him, wrapped him in the biggest hug I could manage. If jealousy could maintain a physical form, I have no doubt it would have burst out of that office and eaten me alive.

"Ugh," Patty grumbled, disgusted at what had just transpired before her. "Let's go," she snarled to the others, and they each gave me, Tex, my friends, and their boyfriends the most hateful look teenage girls could muster.

"Excuse us!" Cassey bellowed after them. She slammed her locker shut and shoved her bag and books into Derek's arms. "Who lit the fuse on her tampon today? I mean, it's only the first day of school. Isn't there a start time for when you can be an official wretch of a human being?"

"I think Patty has an all-day, every-day pass." Amber groaned, rolling her eyes for emphasis.

Tex looked back at the other girls and then turned to me.

"What am I missing?" he asked.

I smiled up at him. He was so clueless and everything I'd ever wanted. "Nothing important," I told him, "just your real-life high school tricks, hating on everyone and everything. I'm pretty sure you've seen their characterizations depicted in at least one movie or TV show in your lifetime."

He grabbed my things from me, and we began walking down the halls.

"Ah, yes, the *'too easies for mesies'*!"

We all laughed loudly at his turn of phrase, and our laughter continued into our homeroom classes. There were three *"unimpressed with our antics"* teachers that morning, but they didn't seem irritated enough to punish us for it.

Blessings rained down as Tex had five of seven classes with me. The only two we didn't have together were his A.F.T. class for football, at which time I was in choir, and his regular English class. I had C.P. English. This class was the only one in which he was with Patty and her skanks.

Thankfully, Cassey takes general English as well, and I knew I could count on her to keep the lions at bay.

For the first few months of the school year, everything was heavenly bliss. I mean, I don't see how things could have gotten much better. Tex made the football team. He was so good that they replaced the current quarterback with him. Trey wasn't upset about it, though; he was one of those all-around athletes who would excel at whatever position you placed him in. When the roster was finalized, he clapped Tex on the shoulder and said, "Alright, cowboy, you throw it, and I'll take care of the rest!"

The very first game was a win, and it was the loudest I had ever cheered. Right after that game, we all met up at the local Dairy Barn where we'd laugh and talk until they eventually had to toss us out, but politely, of course. This became a tradition of sorts, and I'm pretty sure it was one the DB staff could have done without. Most of them were good sports about it, though. It was after the first outstanding football victory, when he drove me home and walked me up to the door, that he slowly slid his hands onto my neck and tilted my head up to look at his face.

"I do love those big brown eyes." He whispered, looking down at me while gently pulling me close and covering my lips with his own.

A buzz like electricity tingled from my calves, up my thighs, and I ashamedly admit, straight into my do-dah. Goosebumps erupted on my arms, and I shivered slightly. Truly, it was only a few minutes, but it felt like an eternity. When he pulled away from me, his gray eyes were hooded and smoky. He cleared his throat to find his voice.

"Are you cold?" he asked.

I smiled against his lips. "No, not cold. Just…happy."

He smiled back and kissed me again. I didn't want to leave him that night, but the parental practice of flicking the porch light ended things for us. We said goodnight, and I watched him climb into his car and drive away.

When I entered the house, my parents were in the living room, whispering about who was going to flick the light next and what other mischievous things they could do. I had to chuckle as I called out to them.

"I can hear you in there."

"No, you can't," my dad answered back, making Mom laugh hysterically.

I shook my head. "Goodnight parents," I said, making my way up the stairs.

"Goodnight, daughter." They called back, still giggling.

four

HOMECOMING: OUR FIRST BUMP IN THE ROAD

W e had officially been a couple for almost three months when it was time for Homecoming. Let me just say that I know every school has a big hoorah for this event, but Saint C. Soldiers outdo them all. Even our teachers, parents, and local businesses get in on the festivities. The big event takes up the whole week and ends with a parade and carnival. The dance is the night before the final ceremonies. We play our biggest rival, the Toledo Tornadoes, in Friday's game and have a roaring bonfire afterward. I don't think the whole place sleeps more than two or three hours a night all week long. Tex was beside himself in amazement. He told us all when we were hanging out one night about how at his old school there was simply a spirit week, a game, and a formal dance. He couldn't believe how every day there was a new event and how the businesses all around were giving the team free meals and merchandise while wishing them luck in the big game. Pete and Derek, who had now become best buds with Tex, enjoyed taking him everywhere and showing him the perks of being a soldier. While they goofed around visiting stores and shop owners, we girls went to work on finding the perfect home-coming dress.

After hitting the usual spots for dresses, we decided to try a new place at one of the outlet malls. The store had two levels, one for formal fancy occasion dresses and the other for wedding dresses and attire. We went to work, finding our sizes and listening to the squeaking sound of hangers over metal rods as we eyed the possibilities. Cassey was being a little too bossy by shooting down a dress Amber or I would pull out by snatching it from us and placing it back on the rack with a "NO". It was fine, though; we just laughed at her. If either of us had been psyched about any of the dresses she vetoed, we would have argued with her and kept them.

Cass's eyes lit up, and I gasped as Amber stepped out of her dressing room to show us the beautiful golden yellow dress she found on the exit rack. That's where they always put last season's dresses that didn't sell, so you can get them for a really good price.

"Oh, Amber," I cooed, "it's like that dress was made for you."

Cassey just gave a nod of agreement. Amber was a petite girl everywhere apart from her chest, which made shopping for clothes a bit of a pain for her. But it seems luck was on her side today. The bottom portion of the dress was made of two layers of fabric. The bottom layer was solid under the sheer outer layer that would sway as she walked. The top was a halter design where the straps sat squarely on the shoulders. Just below the chest, the material split like two sections of fabric, wrapping around and tying up into a bow at her waist in the back. Just the slightest amount of skin could be seen in between the wrappings.

She squealed with delight as she twirled before the three-way mirror.

That left the two of us to try and find our perfect dress. Cassey tossed aside several pieces Amber and I thought would be gorgeous on her, but for Cass, it has to be an absolute for her or it isn't happening. She finally settled on a strapless peacock blue number that split between her breasts and continued down into a V-shape, making a point at the waist. It created a beautiful effect at the place where the material gathered. A sparkling gem lay with tendrils of golden, glittering vines climbing over the bodice. We didn't need to compliment her. She informed us of how good she looked.

I ended up saying yes to the spaghetti-strapped, shimmering white-gold dress that had been displayed on the mannequin when we first walked in. The dress clung to my curves and hips, stopping just below my mid-thigh. I have to admit that, with my long, curly hair hanging down and a pair of to-die-for heels, this dress was a bit, well, sexy. I blushed, realizing that having Tex in my life was changing more than just my relationship status.

The three of us left the shop in good spirits, ready to find some food and talk about the men in our lives. I was finally going to get to take part in the "my boyfriend" conversations.

Is this whole romance and cheerfulness sounding too good to be true? Well, you just hang in there. You'll shortly realize just how right you are.

———

Tex invited me to his house for dinner on the night before the homecoming dance. He wanted me to meet his parents so they would know who, in his words, the "stunning beauty" in the pictures would be. I agreed, but in all honesty, I was petrified. He had met my parents plenty of times, and since my dad was a huge football fan, he loved having Tex in the living room talking football while watching it on the television. Dad even made him help at the grill a couple of times. Mom was completely sold on him from day one.

"My, my Selena," she purred at me. "You better lock that one down. It seems you've won the prize."

I gave her a playful shove after that remark, even though I agreed. It was easy to be with Tex and my parents, but I had no clue how to be with him and his parents. We weren't poor people by any means, but we certainly weren't rich oil heirs either. The closer the time came to meeting them, the more I felt like I was shrinking and running out of air. When the day finally arrived, I had started getting ready around one in the afternoon, and when he arrived at five to pick me up, I was still trying to get myself situated. My mom came into the bathroom, sat me back on the toilet, and looked me dead in the eyes.

"Selena Marie," she stated firmly, "I have not raised you to second-guess yourself or your worth. That young man down there is crazy about you, and you can't take your eyes off of him. Now he wants you to meet his parents, and just like you were excited for us to get to know him, you owe him that same courtesy. You are going to get up, give your face a final touch, and then get your fanny down there and in that car. You are the most amazing young lady on this planet, and now his parents will get to know that as well."

She hugged me and pulled me to my feet. "I'll see you down there," she said, leaving the bathroom.

I looked at myself in the mirror. My hair was pulled up in a loose twist and flowing around my face. My make-up was the earth tones I loved. I twisted my lip gloss and gave a final coat to my lips before popping them together. I took one last look at myself before, with a deep breath, I walked out of the bathroom door and made my way downstairs. It was the smell of Tex's cologne that relaxed me the most. I could breathe him in forever. The scent wasn't too strong, just enough to catch a whiff as the breeze blew or when I hugged him close. It was warm, inviting, and mostly just intoxicating. I breathed him in as he led me to the car, and I would have been perfectly happy to just spend the whole evening with him there. But before I knew it, we were turning into his driveway. Suddenly, my nerves were twisting like Chubby Checker was giving them a personal concert. I swallowed and blinked.

His house was *HUGE*!

It wasn't huge like comically or grossly either, like a bunch of stories high or a maze or whatever. The brick had to have two levels above ground alone. The garage was apart from the home, but it had an attachment, and some steps led above it to what, I assumed, was an apartment of sorts. The front of the house had four large columns that went from roof to porch, and there were semicircular steps leading down to the driveway. The driveway was a wrap-around, so you could drive in one direction and out the other. I counted a total of eight windows in the front, with a small fenced balcony jutting over the door that was supported by the two middle columns. My eyes must have been saucers, and I had to have been making some sort of noise because Tex laughed when he spoke to me.

"Alright now, it's not that big a deal."

I snorted and looked at him, giving him an, "*Are you kidding me?*"

He laughed again at my expression. "No, seriously, it's not like Kim and Kanye's mansion or anything."

I looked out the window at the house again. "It's not like my little humble home either," I mumbled. This is where my insecurities began. As I took in his home and surroundings, I started to categorize the differences between our lives. Questions started forming in my mind, like, "*What if it's just me because I was the first girl he met here? Do I think this kind of life is a future for someone like me?*" These words nagged at my conscience, and my distress was obviously starting to show outwardly because when he parked, he grabbed my hand, squeezing it. I turned my attention back to his handsome face.

"Hey, you," he said, as his hand was pulling me toward him.

I came willingly his way. "Yeah?"

His hand caressed my face, and I placed my hand over it, leaning into his palm. He watched me with that twinkle in his eyes as he pulled me in for a kiss. It relaxed me. He gave my hand one more squeeze and winked at me.

"Come on, beautiful," he said.

My amazement at the outside of the house intensified when we went inside. The ceiling seemed to go up forever, and the staircase to the upstairs was massive and twisted as it made its way to the second floor. The entrance floor was marble, and it clicked with the sound of my heels. If he thought the inside would make me more comfortable, he was mistaken. I felt like an intruder despite being invited by the people who lived there. I was so not used to the lap of luxury!

Tex took my jacket and handbag and placed them on a table under a decorative mirror by the front door. In no time at all, and before I could fully prepare myself, we were entering a beautiful sitting room where a gorgeous woman with the same sandy blond hair as Tex stood up and walked over towards us. She had a gleaming white smile, and though she was probably as old as my parents, she certainly didn't look like it. There were only faint wrinkle lines around her eyes and mouth. She looked severely elegant in a cream-colored pantsuit. The woman was flawless. As she approached me, I was mentally scolding my stomach, thinking it had better not do that bubbly noise thing because I was nervous. If it embarrassed me in front of his mother, I would refuse to eat for the rest of the week!

"Why, Texas, it's about time," she sang out, making her way to us.

I wasn't aware of how hard I was holding Tex's hand until he squeezed me back with a little shake of our hands. "I'm sorry," I whispered to him. He chuckled and maneuvered us to his mother.

"Mom, I would like you to meet Selena."

"Selena," she said, making my name snake out of her mouth. She gave another dazzling smile.

"Aren't you a beauty? I'm so sorry Texas has taken his sweet old time getting us introduced and all."

"Oh, thank you, Mrs. Conrad, and it's alright... I mean, he just met my parents recently, and..."

"Nonsense child," she interrupted. "I happen to know how much my little Texas adores your mother and father. He never shuts up about you all when he sits to have talks with me."

I looked at him and smiled. He smiled back at me and then cleared up any confusion by telling me how drinking sweet tea either out in the gazebo or on a porch swing somewhere and talking with his mother was just something they had always done.

"It is," she confirmed as she took me by the arm and started leading me back across the entryway and into the big room at the right of the house.

"Texas is my only son, and he is the light of my life, you

see." She told me along the way, "Why, I make him tell me everything I can get out of him. Y'all kids just grow up too fast, and we parents need anything we can get to hang on to for as long as we can."

When we made it to the large cherry wood dining table, she instructed Tex to get my chair, as she had raised him to do so. My senses were being overworked by the symphony of different smells wafting through the air. Some delicious food was being prepared, and that mixed with the vanilla sugar cookie smell of the room itself, was pure bliss.

"Yes, ma'am," he told her while pulling out my chair. He then went to the seat at the end of the table in front of the window and held it out for his mother, who thanked him. Once she was settled, he took the seat across from me. Mere moments after we had all put napkins in our laps, two ladies started bringing out drinks and food.

"I apologize for my husband's absence, dear," his mother began telling me amidst the movement of arms and dishes. "He is a businessman, as I'm sure you know, and we're lucky half the time to see him at all, let alone at the dinner table."

"Oh, it's alright…"

"Don't you worry a bit about tonight; however, I have instructed Mr. Conrad to have his utterly pale keister down at this table or else!"

Both Tex and I snickered at her comment, which got another glowing smile from her for the both of us.

She had just finished asking me all about my life, family, school, and extracurricular activities when there was a grunt from a door at the back of the room. It swung open, and an older but still handsome version of Tex came into the room. He had a scowl on his slightly wrinkled face. He was about an inch or two taller than Tex, but I suspected that Tex would have a growth spurt somewhere before the age of nineteen. His eyes were a piercing blue, and they struck each of us in our pupils before settling back on his wife. He gave a nod of his head, jerked his chair away from the table, and sat. In a gruff voice, he called back into the kitchen.

"Dang it to all, I'm here, Gretch… Could I, *NOW*, have my dinner?"

One of the women, the short one with salt and pepper hair, who had already served us, bustled out of the kitchen with food and drink. She had a smug look on her face and didn't even pretend to care that the master of the house had just yelled at her.

"I told ya upstairs in your office, Mr. Conrad, that Mrs. Conrad said no dining for you in there today. You are to sit at the table. So here you sit, and now you may have your food."

His face reddened, and he shot Mrs. Conrad a look when she failed to suppress a giggle over the bite of food she was taking. He cleared his throat and slapped the napkin on his lap.

"So it seems," he growled.

Gretch gave an "mm-hmm" of agreement and saun-tered back through the door in which she had come. Mr. Conrad began shoveling food into his mouth.

"T.C.," Mrs. Conrad said to him, "have you forgotten your manners or are you once again just choosing to ignore them?"

He looked at her while chewing, then finally swallowed. Wiping his mouth with the napkin, he turned to me. I believe that if I had been able to move at all, I would have been reduced to a puddle under the table at the look he gave me.

He took a deep breath and sighed before holding out his hand to me. "Texas Conrad the Third," he said.

I reached out my hand to him. "Selena Ayers," I said softly in return.

"Ayers!" he bellowed, shoveling in another mouthful. "Aren't those gypsy people?" he asked.

Tex choked on his drink, and his mother dropped her fork loudly while giving her husband a fierce look. He finished chewing and was getting a drink when he noticed his wife.

"What?" he asked, brows furrowing down as if he were confused as to why she would be seething.

She took a deep breath, composing herself, before addressing me. "I do apologize, Selena. Mr. Conrad can be a bit gruff at times. It's the businessman in him. Please excuse his inappropriate comment." She smiled at me before giving her husband another withering look.

Tex cleared his throat this time. "Hey Dad," he said, "Selena and I are attending the Homecoming dance together tomorrow. Mother is going to take some pictures here before we drive to school. Would you be able to meet with us for a bit as well?"

"Homecoming?" his father asked, "Is it that time already, boy? I told you I wanted to know the details of every football game. Why haven't I heard about this before now?"

"T.C." Tex's mother cut in. "You will calm yourself at once. Tex has told you about this numerous times. I've told you before, you need to get yourself another one of those ridiculous small black books so you can keep as much track of your son as you do your businesses."

"Amelia, I do keep track of my son," he argued back. "Do I not buy his football gear, get him specialized training sessions, or have I not been aware of him dating this gypsy girl since the summer?" He finished his comment by opening his palm and flinging it towards me in a gesture.

"T.C.!" she shrieked.

"Oh goodness!" He grunted, slinging down his fork and turning to me. "Are you offended in any way, child? Do you not know Ayers is the name of a famous gypsy man? Would you like me to no longer mention your heritage while you are here?"

His words were blunt and quick. He was so unlike Tex that I could hardly believe it was his father. My stomach decided that it would now do whatever it pleased, no matter what threat I made. As I felt the tension knot below, I blinked and stammered just once before answering to the best of my ability.

"I... I'm fine, sir. I am aware that I am of Romanian gypsy descent. However, I have no idea how many great-grandfathers ago that particular Ayers had been."

"There!" T.C. said abruptly while addressing his wife, "She's not offended in the least."

He picked up his fork and went back to mauling his food. I looked over at Tex, who lifted his mouth in that crooked smile and winked at me. For the remainder of the meal and into dessert, I kept my hand pressed firmly against my stomach; we would fight this out to the end! Mr. Conrad informed Tex all about the latest deals and work going into the stations and how things had progressed. A few times, Mrs. Conrad would interject and explain some-thing he was talking about to me, and I would feign interest and nod. Plates were being cleared when, afraid I could no longer stave off the angry grumblings of my digestive system, I excused myself to the restroom. Mrs. Conrad instructed Gretch to show me where to go while both Mr. Conrad and Tex stood as I exited the room. On my way to the restroom, I marveled at how Mr. Conrad at least seemed to have some semblance of manners, even if he was altogether rude.

Inside the enormous restroom, I allowed my complaining insides to have at it. An orchestra playing various tunes of bubbles and gurgles ensued. I took this time to think about the events at the table. While I wasn't attacked and was truly not offended, I still couldn't help feeling somewhat frightened by his father's brusque treatment of me. In a way, I felt as if he was almost disappointed.

With a huge breath, I brushed these feelings away and washed my hands. Looking at my reflection in the mirror, I began to scold myself. How could I think his father was disappointed? I mean, he didn't even know me, and in this day and age, were there still people out there who would let what they "thought" they knew about a person's name or history be a deciding factor in whether or not they liked them? Thinking about all of this was making the somewhat loosened knot in my stomach work back towards being imprisoned and, not wanting to relive that nightmare, I dried my hands and stepped out the door.

Heading back out, I feared I was going to get lost and be unable to find my way back. Twice I went back to the bathroom door and looked around before seeing the sparkling vase of orchids I had passed on the way here. Just ahead was the entryway which would lead me to the middle sitting room before the dining room. My shoe clicks were muted as I stepped on the soft carpet. The raised voices caused me to stop in my tracks before slowly easing closer so I could make out what they were saying.

"You don't even know her dad. You've barely spoken to her since you came in here," Tex was saying.

"I don't have to spend a lot of time speaking to someone to know them, Texas, and you, as my son, should know that. I am a businessman, and I can tell what a person is about in less than three words. Gypsies are notorious gold diggers and thieves. They are all alike, and the women are worse than the men. They'll entice you with those chocolate eyes and dance for you. Oh yes," his father was arguing, "and then they'll wipe your pockets clean while you sleep."

My hand came up to my mouth as I gasped. I couldn't believe what I was hearing. I had never done anything to this man, and my family doesn't even embrace our heritage like that for goodness sake.

Tex's mother came to my defense. "Oh, good heavens, T.C. You think everybody in the world is after money. What about me then you old coot? You married me, and I wasn't the richest thing in the world now, was I? You sound ridiculous, and you had better not say a single harsh word to that young lady. Do you understand me?"

"Oh, hush it, Amelia," T.C. grunted. "I'm not gonna say a cross word to that girl, but I am going to say this to you, Tex. You can go ahead and date that pretty girl. I'm not blind, and I can see her beauty and understand your interest, but you remember this above all else. You are a Texas Conrad young man. You have expectations passed down to you that you will not ignore. Go on and date her," he exclaimed while rising from the table. Then he pointed his finger at Tex and finished by saying, "You will not get attached, though. Do you hear me talking to you? You are not to get anywhere close to thinking this will be anything more than it already is."

Tex opened his mouth to argue, but his dad's stern look and second point of the finger shut him up. "Not a single word," he told him.

"Where are you going, T.C.?" Amelia demanded of her husband. "The young lady hasn't even made it back yet. You can't just leave."

"I've got work to do, Amelia." He barked, and then turned and went to the door.

"Texas Conrad the Third!" she bellowed after him, but the sound of the swinging door was the only response she received.

She and Tex were now talking more quietly with one another, and since I couldn't hear what they were saying, I gave a small cough before making my way fully into the room. I entered, each of them adjusting in their seats and smiling at me.

"Darlin'," Mrs. Conrad said to me, "T.C. apologizes, but he's had to get upstairs to the office on account of some business."

She was getting up, and Tex was already out of his seat and making his way to me.

I smiled as if everything in the world was perfect. "That's alright, Mrs. Conrad. I understand."

"Please, dear," she cooed, giving me a quick hug and pushing me back from her. She held my shoulders in her hands and looked at me. "You call me Amelia, alright? And don't you go being a stranger! You are welcome here anytime, you hear?"

"Yes, ma'am."

She let go of me and hugged her son, talking in his ear. "She is a beauty, Texas. Now you make sure to take good care of her."

"I will, momma."

She told us goodnight and disappeared through the entryway.

We were left standing there. I could feel tension in the air and was going to try and say something, anything, to abate it, but Tex beat me to it.

He grabbed my hand. "Wanna see where I live?" he asked.

I looked at him, utterly confused. "Um… I'm in your house. Isn't this where you live?"

He chuckled adorably. "Come on, follow me."

I was led through another door from the dining room and down a back hallway that opened up into a glassed-in sunroom. It was furnished with wicker furniture and over-stuffed pillows. There were small shelves filled with books and a porch swing hanging just in front of the backyard area. Tex opened a door that led outside to the steps I had seen before. We walked up to a deck area and inside the attachment. I was right about it being an apartment above the garage.

"Welcome to Casa de Tex!" he said, laughing.

I looked around. I could see him everywhere. To the left of me was a small kitchen area with a little counter and stools. To the right was an open living room space. It was small, but there was a sofa, a recliner, and a large television with numerous game systems on a stand under the flat screen. Directly in front of me were steps that led down into an open bedroom. He had a large sleigh bed that you walked straight to once you were at the bottom of the stairs. There was a walk-in closet to the left of the bed area, and to the right at the back was a door that led into a bath-room. The whole place was super clean and smelled like his cologne.

"Well?" he asked me. "What do you think?"

I laughed. "Obviously, I think you're the luckiest teenager on earth to have so much privacy and convenience."

"You use big words too much." He said as he leapt up, jumping onto the bed.

"I do not!"

He looked at his phone, then rose and snatched me

down onto the bed facing him. "I have you all to myself for a couple of hours."

I giggled as he put his lips on mine. We continued like that, kissing over and over again and then talking and laughing before falling back into deep kisses for the rest of our time together.

Oh, the bliss I was in. This is what I had been missing all along. Feeling wanted and having a boyfriend. Sadly, it is true that time flies when you are having fun. It seemed like barely a moment had passed when he let out an irritated groan.

"Time to drive you home," he complained, rising and pulling me from the bed. I smoothed my dress down and grabbed my things. I noticed him staring at me and furrowed my eyebrows, wondering what was wrong.

"I don't think I've told you this today, but I want to make sure I do. You are the most beautiful girl I have ever seen."

I felt heat from a blush creeping into my cheeks. "Tex," I said quietly as I went to him and kissed him as passionately as I knew how. He broke from me after a few minutes and murmured that he, unfortunately, had to get me home because he had promised my father.

We rode home in silence, listening to his playlist with me singing along here and there. Just before we arrived on my street, Tex turned down the radio.

"So…what do you think of my parents?" he asked.

"Your mother is so wonderful, and you look a lot like your father," I added.

Tex just nodded, so I continued.

"You have your mother's hair, though."

"Did you like my father as well?" he asked.

I blinked and fidgeted with my dress hem. "I like him well enough, but…"

"But…" he urged.

"But… I… I don't think your father likes me very much."

He let out a knowing sigh. "Selena, please don't let that gypsy nonsense sway you at all. My father prides himself on knowing all about history, ancestry, important events and so on. He uses his knowledge as a conversation starter in his deals. Plus, he's dead set on his ways. He was raised a certain way, and he does all he can to try and raise me under those same beliefs and ideals. Thankfully, my mother has a better head on her shoulders and does all she can to correct anything she believes my father is teaching me that is detrimental to my character."

I nodded my head, hoping I was convincing him that I understood, but just between you and me, it sounded a whole lot like he was saying his father is prejudiced, and I didn't understand that at all. I have always determined how well I liked a person based on who they were to me, not their background, color, or anything else for that matter.

We pulled into my driveway, and he turned off the car before turning to face me.

"Something is wrong, isn't it?" he asked.

I shook my head but he stopped the movement by grabbing my face gently.

"Selena, you and I have a good thing going on here. I don't want it ruined with secrets and lies. Please tell me. What's wrong?"

There was a warm puddle of tears forming on my bottom lids. I didn't want to mess up anything between us, and I had no idea what words I could say that would make everything still be alright. But then, as I looked up at him and saw such concern for me, I couldn't hold back the words.

"I… I heard your father talking to you when I came

back from the bathroom. I didn't mean to eavesdrop, but I did. I promise, I was just unable to move."

"Selena…" Tex whispered, imploring me.

I shook my head. "No," I said, "it's alright. I mean, just as you said to him, he doesn't know me, and I'm sure he was just using what knowledge he has to protect his son."

Tex moved quickly out of the car and came around to my side. He opened the door and pulled me out, enveloping me in his arms and hugging me close.

"Selena," he said, gently pulling me back to look at me. "Listen to me, alright? I am so sorry you heard that, and I am so sorry for my father's words and behavior. Please don't let this take anything away from us."

I let out a sob and laughed which sounded more like a drunken hiccup. "What are we to do then?" I asked, "Your father says that this is to be nothing more than it is."

He took both my hands in his and shrank down to meet my eyes. I looked back at him.

"I am not my father, Selena. I love him and I respect him, yes, but he is constantly wrapped up in his career. If you didn't notice, he bellowed about not being kept up on my football, but let me ask you this. How many games have you seen him attend?"

I thought for a moment before answering. "I don't recall seeing him at any of them. I mean, now that I know what he looks like and all. I believe I would have noticed him."

"Of course you would have." Tex agreed. "You haven't seen him because he never comes. He doesn't even know I'm the quarterback." Tex laughed and said, "I don't want you to think a second more about anything he said or did tonight. My mother adores you, and so do I. One day, he will too. I know it."

I nodded my head and gave him a squeeze, which he

returned. At the door to my house, he kissed me deeply and told me how he couldn't wait to see me in my dress for the dance. I gave him another kiss and said goodnight as I went into the house.

It was probably a few minutes later than I expected before I heard the car start and drive away. I wondered if he was taking breaths and thinking of everything that had happened the same way I was.

five

SAME FATHER, DIFFERENT TOWN

Out in his car, after pulling out into the street and heading toward home, he was doing just that. Tex was taking deep breaths, long deep breaths, and doing his best to compose himself. What I didn't know was that his father had always been this way, and apparently it has been a problem more often than not. Quite a few times the family missed out on what would have been very lucrative business deals because, in one case, his father found out that the C.E.O. was of Jewish descent, and that meant there was some ridiculous reason not to trust him. Another was a merger that fell through because the controlling interest in the merging company belonged to a woman. Over the years, Tex has always had to make sure the people he hangs out with pass muster to avoid the embarrassment they would have to endure should his father find some flaw with the individual. What happened at dinner wasn't Tex's fault at all, but he was blaming himself. He should have done some research or something to spare me his father's ill will, but he was just so head over heels for me that he didn't give it a second thought. What kind of person studies names and heritages just so they can use the information as a means for judgment and business deals? As soon as Tex's car drove onto the interstate, he slammed the palm of his hand twice against the steering wheel and cursed bitterly. He had no idea how he was going to make everything work out between us with his dad being the belligerent, judgmental jerk he's always been.

And then there's Vanessa. Ever since Tex was in grade school, her parents were accepted among the social elite within his parental cluster. Vanessa Marrow. For as long as he could remember, she has always been present somewhere in his life. When they were younger, in middle school, his father and hers would talk about how great it would be when their two children were married and had children of their own to carry on the family businesses. Back then, Tex was all for it. Vanessa was attractive, and he was a teenage boy with teenage hormones, so why not date the little vixen and conquer that masculine hurdle? And he did just that one evening when they were supposedly studying for a geometry test. It was around a year later when the two of them just fizzled out. They would still go on dates, and anytime her father came to his home or his father went to theirs, the two of them would hang out together, sometimes doing that one thing just to have something to do. It seemed they were both aware that they were going through the motions to avoid having to deal with their respective fathers, but Tex never broached the subject with her, and she never indicated so to him. Sometimes he wondered if she was in love with him, though, because he'd seen her mother with her dad plenty of times, and it seemed that the woman was just as uninterested in her husband as Vanessa sometimes seemed to be towards him. Maybe that was how the women in their family were.

That mental dilemma was another reason why Tex had

been so gung-ho about this move to Saint Caine. He was going to get an opportunity to start fresh and have a viable excuse for why he and Vanessa just seemed to drift apart. Meeting me was the icing on the cake for him. I was someone he knew he wanted to have a relationship with, someone he wanted more than just to check something off of his list of things to do. He knew his father was a bigot and prejudiced, but he hadn't realized until tonight just how much his father's opinions were going to decide his future. Arriving at his home, he smacked the steering wheel once more and swore. What was he going to do about this? Was there anything he could do?

When he got back home, he found his mother in the sun-room gently swaying back and forth in the cushioned swing. Every piece of furniture in this room was white wicker, even the swing. She held up a glass of sweet tea when he stepped down into the room as a sort of "hello". He chuckled, making his way to take up the other end of the oscillating couch on chains.

"Are you sure you don't need anything stronger after tonight?" he asked, eyebrows raised as he nodded toward the glass.

"What makes you think this isn't a long island?" she retorted, giving him a look that acknowledged that they both knew what a dreadful ogre his father could be.

"I couldn't blame you if it was."

"Mm-hmm," was her only response as she brought the glass to her painted peach lips for another swallow.

They sat in blissful silence for a spell before Tex finally struck up the nerve to ask his mother for advice.

"What am I going to do?"

She didn't need him to elaborate. The two of them were as close as a mother and son could be. She knew when he was happy, angry, and sad. A long sigh escaped her.

"What is there to do, son? This man isn't going to change anytime soon. I wish I could tell you otherwise, but we both know I'd be lying."

"But why, Mother?" Tex protested, snagging the chain of the swing with his hand as he dipped his head back in defeat. "I mean, I know that even though this is the twenty-first century, there are plenty of uptight well-to-dos that thrive on believing themselves to be an elite upper class, but is it still so bad that my relationship with a girl who just happens to be of a once taboo ancestry could affect the affairs of my entire family?"

She turned to give him that small smile. The smile she reserved for when she was apologizing for her husband without vocally saying the words. "It shouldn't, dear, and I wish I could tell you he's full of it, but I've met these people he deals with, and I've seen their disgusting prejudices and self-exaltation with my own eyes. I've heard their vulgar insults with my own ears. It's pathetic and heartbreaking, and when I think about all that you've had to endure because of it..."

She didn't finish the sentence; she just pursed her lips and shook her head. After a moment, she reached out, grabbed his hand, and squeezed. He could see fresh tears gathering at her lashes.

"Sometimes," she whispered, just loud enough for the two of them to hear, "I truly wish I had taken you and left. I should have just grabbed our things and taken off without looking back."

"Mom, hey," Tex soothed, pulling on the hand that was wrapped up in his, "don't think like that. You have always been the best mom anyone could ever hope for."

She snorted a laugh, which made him smile as he kept assuring her. "I mean it," he said sternly, "if you had left then you would have had to work, and I'm not saying that you couldn't, but I am going to put out that we would not have had the life we are accustomed to."

"Wouldn't happiness and freedom make up for that?"

It would, but telling her that would only make her feel worse. Instead, he just squeezed her hand and stared off into the distance.

Later on that evening, as he lay in bed, the black satin sheets crumpled and lay at his bare waist. His muscled arms were stretched behind his head as he lay against the cool pillow beneath them. His eyes were open, looking out at the starlit sky above. There were so many thoughts of ways that he could keep me and our relationship, but still make his father happy and avoid any family drama. Truth be told, he only needed to keep things on the down low until after his father managed a merger. After that, it shouldn't matter who he chooses to associate with. Feeling that it may just be the answer he was looking for, he breathed contentedly and closed his eyes to sleep.

six

THE DANCE AND ALL THAT

After the parental dinner, the whole affair slowly faded from our minds. Tex, Pete, and Derek arranged for a car and picked me, Cass, and Amber up from my house. We all went to Tex's house, and I listened to the gang *ooh* and *ahh* at the home and all its beauty. Amelia was beside herself with glee, taking pictures of all of us. The best shots came from us girls standing on the balcony over the door and the guys holding our flowers up to us as we looked down on them. It was like a scene from a movie of the guys trying to court their crushes. We ate at the fanciest restaurant in Saint Caine. It was a place called *The Plaza*, and it was a four-star hotel that housed the restaurant on its top floor. We sat by a window where we could look out and see the dazzling lights of the boardwalk and watch the moonlight glisten on the ocean water in the distance. We all ate and groaned over the exquisite taste and texture of the expensive food before heading to the dance with fully satisfied bellies. The night was wonderful up until the crowning ceremonies. Naturally, the "*ho patrol*" all put their names in for the queen and ended up being the homecoming court to Patty's Royal Highness. Neither I nor my friends cared, as we refused to subject ourselves to the popularity game. The only problem with this was that the homecoming king was selected by all the names on the football team. Can you guess who was voted as king? That's right... My Tex.

Why is that such a problem? You might ask. Well, I'll tell you, or maybe you've already guessed. The homecoming king and queen share a dance. The last thing any girl at Saint C. wants is for her man to have to be anywhere near Patty *"Put her hands on your man"* Kearns. As if I wasn't furious enough, Cassey's rebel alter ego was rearing its ugly head as well.

"Are you freaking kidding me?" Cassey spat. "She probably rigged the freaking votes, the skank twat!"

"Cass!" Amber protested.

"What?" Cass argued back at her. "You know I'm probably right!"

"Well yes," Amber begrudgingly agreed, "but you don't have to let yourself be so crass. I mean, you have so much more class than that."

Cassey's answer was to shrug and crack her knuckles.

"It'll be fine," I groaned while rolling my eyes. "It's just a dance, guys; no big deal." I knew it was best to brush it off this way; otherwise, we would be bailing Cass out of jail tonight.

"Mm-hmm," they both hummed at me while staring daggers at Patty.

Patty made a big show of smiling at me while placing her arms around Tex's neck. He, and God love him for this, pulled down her arms and made some room between them by grabbing one of her hands off his shoulder and placing just one hand on her side. She smiled like this was fine, but I could tell she was seething inside. No boy rejected the queen bee of Saint Caine.

"Tex?" she said to him.

"Yeah?" he answered.

"Why are you wasting your time with Selena?" she asked, blinking her falsies at him.

He started to answer, but she interrupted him with a voice of mock concern. "I mean… I get that she's pretty and all. She makes good grades and everything, but you, Tex, *YOU* are the freaking quarterback of a championship football team. You are the heir of a wealthy family. And sure, she's somewhat popular, but you should be dating the homecoming queen, the prom queen, the elite."

"You sound like my father." He snapped at her.

"Well, isn't that a good thing?" She pleaded with him. "Your father, above all, would know what is best for you."

She jerked her hand from his and pushed herself against him, snaking her arms around his neck and speaking into his ear.

"Look handsome. You did well; you came to a new school and found an attractive enough girl to claim your place. But it's been long enough. You're established. It's time to move up the ladder. Besides, Saint Selena isn't going to let you get anywhere near her panties. Whereas I," she said, moving closer to his ear, "aren't even wearing any."

With the last of her words, she touched her tongue to his ear and nipped him with her teeth. He jerked back from her and stared down into her face. She blinked at him innocently. "Something wrong, lover?" she asked.

"This dance is over." He stated firmly, wiping his ear off as he made his way through the crowd.

Patty looked after him. "For now, anyway." She called out and waved her hand.

Tex was borderline furious as he approached the table. Amber and Pete were on the floor dancing, and Cassey was the only one sitting there.

"Where's Derek?" he asked her.

Cassey shrugged. "I don't know and don't care right now. He's being a douche."

Tex rolled his eyes at this. He'd realized over the months that I was right about the volatile relationship between Cass and Derek. It was best to just let them do their thing. He jerked the crown off his head and put it on the table. After looking around, he spoke to Cass again.

"Selena... Do you know where she is?"

Cassey snorted dramatically. "Of course I do. I'm her best friend." She rolled her eyes, grabbing a toothpick off the table and slinging it into her mouth. "She took off to the bathroom when Patty started getting too fresh with you. She said she couldn't watch that. I offered to hit Patty hard enough to make her show us her dinner, but Selena refuses to let me get physical at school."

Tex didn't catch the end of what Cassey was saying. He was already speeding his way to the ladies' room and managed to reach the door just as I was coming out. He caught my arms and turned me to him.

"Are you alright?" he asked me.

I looked up and saw that same concern that was there the night we discussed his father. I gave him a reassuring smile.

"Yes, I'm fine." I told him. "It is much better to take a bathroom break than to get kicked out of the school and possibly suffer punishments for drowning the *Ho*-coming queen in the punch bowl."

Tex laughed, and I joined him. He pulled me into his arms and kissed me. "You want to get out of here now?"

"I would love that."

We all piled into the car and decided to head to Cassey's. Her house had direct access to the beach, and we loved to have bonfires there well into the night. Her parents got us a bunch of snacks, and we played music as we talked. Tex had the guys roaring in laughter by telling him about his potential dance rape.

"What the heck, man?" Derek gaffed at him. "You mean she truly, *actually*, said that to you?"

"No way, man!" Pete said, laughing so hard that he choked himself.

"I swear it," Tex said, holding up an open palm. "The girl told me she didn't have any drawers on."

This announcement made Cass, Amber, and I make twisted, wrinkled faces with sounds of disgust, while the boys bellowed even harder.

Tex moved me in front of him, and I backed up against his chest. He was holding me there. We had a soft blanket around us as we leaned against the large rock behind him. It got quiet for a moment, and we were all relaxing.

Then Derek just bellowed out, "*PLEASE*, tell me that all y'all got your underwear on!"

The laughter exploded into the night.

seven

I LOVE YOU

Tex and I continued to grow closer as the year went on. I was at his home several more times after that first visit. While I spent a lot of time with his mother, I still only saw his father two other times. Once, when I was coming into the house as he was leaving. He merely nodded at us and called back for Tex to read the report he put in the den. The second time was Tex's birthday. He came into the room long enough for the presents to be opened. I hadn't even noticed he had left the room when we were gathering up the discarded paper. On Valentine's Day, Tex and I went to a Japanese steak house with our friends. This time, Cassey was with another guy from the football team. His name was Mitch, and he got along well enough with Pete and Tex. We knew he was up to date on Cassey when he told Pete that he was happy to hang out with them until Cass and Derek got back together again. By late April, Mitch was out, and Derek was back.

It was time for prom. Much like homecoming, the girls and I spent weeks going from dress shop to dress shop in search of something perfect. Cassey chose a tight-fitting spaghetti-strapped burgundy dress. It looked lovely with her blond hair and matching lipstick. Amber picked out a two-piece skirt and beaded top ensemble. It was a blue color with swirls of silver, and the skirt portion was made with waves in the material. My dress was chocolate gold. It was one-shouldered and form-fitting. A split went up to my thigh, and my heels were dyed to match. I wore my hair in an elaborate updo with a glittering designer comb holding all of my curls in place. When the boys arrived to pick us up, Tex just stared at me. He stared so long that the others had moved to the car while I was waiting for him to take my hand.

"Tex?" I asked him, furrowing my brows together.

He licked his lips and ran his hand down his mouth. The other hand was in his pocket. A second later, he smiled.

"I didn't think you could be any more beautiful," he said. "But here I am, right now, looking at you and realizing you just get more beautiful every day."

I blushed fiercely, looking down to try and hide the heat in my face. Then I looked up at him.

"Thank you. You are quite handsome yourself." I told him with a girlish giggle.

"You think so?" he asked, taking my hand and leading me to the car.

"Oh yes. I decided that just a few moments ago."

"Well," he said, "lucky me."

We giggled together and climbed into the car.

It was the same routine as the previous dance. Pictures, driving, dancing, laughing, and the bonfire. All of it was the same, except for the short hours between midnight and morning. In those hours, my life would once again change forever.

Tex drove us to his house after we said goodbye to the

others. I was shaking as we moved over to the steps that would lead up to his private room. He had long ago put his jacket around me, but here I was shaking worse now than I was then. My mind was racing, and I was almost certain Tex had to be able to hear my thundering heart.

"You must be freezing." He said while leading me more quickly to the door and inside.

I gave my head a shake. "No, not really," I answered breathily.

He looked at me strangely. I could tell he was a little confused, but then, almost like I could see his thoughts forming, his eyebrows came apart, and his face softened. He shut the door behind us before dropping the keys on the mantle of the fireplace. He grabbed both of my hands up in his, caressing the tops of my palms with his thumbs as he spoke.

"Selena, are you sure?"

Nervous laughter erupted from me. I quickly put my hand to my mouth to stop it. When I gained my composure, I made myself face him fully so that he could see that I was absolutely sure that this was something I wanted. That familiar look of concern was beginning to sharpen his features.

"Don't." I quickly blurted out, "Don't be concerned for me. I am sure."

He licked his lips and nodded once before I led him down the stairs and stopped in front of his bed. He just stood there before me, holding my waist and looking down at me. We kissed deeply a few times. Then, with my eyes locked on his, I pushed his jacket off my shoulders. I saw him swallow hard. A small hiss came from his lips as I moved even closer to him and guided his hand to the zipper at the side of my dress. It gave me courage and a little sense of power, as I felt a slight tremor in his strong hand. He pressed his mouth to mine, beginning another deep, long kiss as he slowly pulled the zipper from top to bottom. My dress fell to the floor, and just moments after that, there was nothing but kisses, breathing, and magic. As I lay under the covers and in his arms, Tex gently stroked my hair and kissed my forehead. His hand stopped for a moment as he spoke quietly in the dark.

"Selena?"

"Yes," I answered drowsily.

"I love you."

His words weren't too quiet or too loud. They were matter-of-fact, and I knew he meant it. I tilted my head up to his as he looked down at me. Hurriedly, he said it again.

"I love you."

"I love you, too," I told him.

Then our lips were together, and the magic began all over again.

True love, soul mates, your other half—whatever you want to call it. That's exactly what Tex and I were. I knew it wholly and irrevocably. After prom night, we continued to deepen our connection with one another. We talked all the time about everything and anything. We laughed so much, and I was so incredibly happy. I believe Tex was too. I have to believe that, but you do remember that at the beginning of this tale, I told you that while it's said the soul mate will be found, it's not guaranteed to have a lifetime of happiness with them. So, as you've probably started to figure out, what I've told you so far must be all the good, happy moments. Well, aside from his father's obvious reluctance to accept our relationship, but still, you know the inevitable is going to happen. What is it? What could go wrong, even despite a father's rejection, that could ever tear apart this obvious, meant-to-be love?

The answer?

The same story that has written tragedies and won Oscars. The same tale that has caused countries to go to war, lies to be told, murder to be committed, and yes, so sadly, love to be lost. A little bit of hatred and a whole lot of greed.

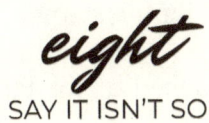

SAY IT ISN'T SO

The first major blow-up happened just after Christmas of our senior year. It started with Tex suddenly not being able to spend as much time with me anymore. His father had decided that with Tex's upcoming graduation, he needed to start focusing more on the business and added that he needed his son's help as the stations that were previously doing phenomenally had now started to plateau. The investments were far from meeting the intended goal and T.C., as Mrs. Conrad calls him, had even gone so far as to suggest a possible bankruptcy if things did not change in the immediate future.

This simply could not happen. Ever since Texas Conrad the First built the original Texacon station, the family has always kept that legacy alive. Texas Conrad the Third refused to be the weak link in a chain of great accomplishments. So... My Tex was hauled into an adult life and mindset a couple of years sooner than he expected to be.

It was late on a Friday night when he arrived at my house. I didn't even know he was there. I was up in my room studying for the A.C.T. when my door opened and he walked in. Naturally, I jumped up from my bed and leapt at him, holding him as close to me as I could. He returned my hug, but I could tell it was half-hearted, and there was something else bothering me. His cologne was there, and it had the familiar smell I was used to, but it wasn't right. There was another mingled in with it. I pulled back from him and looked at his face. He wouldn't meet my eyes.

"What is it?" I asked him.

"What?" he said quickly, then shook his head. "Nothing; there's nothing. I'm fine."

"Tex," I said, in a tone indicating that I knew that there was something wrong.

"Selena, please, can I just be here with you? Please? Just let me be here with you and hold you alright."

He moved to the bed and laid on it. I acquiesced and lay in front of him, letting him put his arm around me. I brushed my fingers through his hair a few times, then I moved up to kiss him, and that's when I caught it. A faint smell of coconut. The kind of scent that someone would have if they'd used tanning lotion earlier in the day or something. Not only was that something to give me pause, but another conundrum followed immediately after. For some reason, his kiss was different. I mean he kissed me back, and they were his lips, but a feeling brushed through me, like the kiss was unsure somehow. As I pulled back, my eyes swept over his face. His own eyes were closed, but his face was contorted, like kissing me was hurting him in some way.

He opened my eyes to find me staring at him.

"Is something wrong?" he asked.

"Yes."

"Well, what is it?"

"I'm not sure." I admitted, pushing back away from him some more. "Tex?" I asked.

"Yeah?"

"Have you been with someone else?"

My question made him jolt up from the bed. He stayed in a sitting position while looking down at me. I couldn't read a single feature on his face for the first time since we'd met. I looked at him expectantly, waiting for his answer.

"How could you ask me that, Selena?" he demanded.

His tone was harsh. It took me back a bit, and I struggled to answer at first. "I… I'm sorry, it's… It's just that I feel; I *felt* like there was something different, and I just blurted out the thought that came to my mind."

"You don't trust me? Is that it?"

I stared at him. I hoped I would; had wanted to see hurt in his face and eyes, but I didn't see that. I didn't see any indication of it, only irritation.

"I trust you, Tex," I said, reaching my hand to his cheek.

"Then what would make you ask me that, huh? What would cause you to say something like that?"

"I'm sorry, I am. I know it's not anything you and I have ever had to deal with, even with all the passes and offers Patty has thrown your way. I shouldn't have asked you that."

I was startled by his anger now. His jaw tightened, and if I hadn't known better, I would have sworn tears were starting to form in his eyes.

"Oh, my goodness, babe, I am so sorry," I told him, touching his hand lightly.

With my last words, he blew out a hard breath, and I was relieved to see his face soften. "I just want to hold you." He said it so quietly and so pleadingly that my heart tugged in my chest.

What could I do? I pulled him back down beside me, turned my back to him, and wrapped myself up in his arms. We didn't talk; we didn't kiss. He just held me. At some point I fell asleep, and when I woke up in the morning, he was gone and had left a note on my pillow.

Thank you for letting me embrace you through the night.

I have to go back home for a bit, but I'll be back to get you around five, and take you out for the evening. I'm thinking of dinner and a movie. I love you.

Tex

I was elated at his note and grateful that I was going to get to spend time with him that I had been missing. By the time Tex arrived to pick me up he was smiling, and he was happy. He was my Tex. His kiss was the kiss I knew and remembered, and I felt my nerves easing as I inhaled his cologne. I pushed all my fears and anxieties aside and enjoyed every minute we spent together.

nine

THAT WAS A CLOSE ONE!

He was so stupid for not taking a shower and changing his clothes before coming to see me. Tex berated himself over and over again for not having the common sense to do just that. He was pacing in his room, holding his hands above his head as he tracked a path back and forth in front of his bed. Of course, his father would delve into his bag of tricks to try and keep Tex in line. If only he had known Vanessa and her family had been invited to dinner that evening, he wouldn't have even shown up. When he had skipped into the dining room earlier, he came to an abrupt halt, his mouth hanging open and confusion etched on his face. When he looked at his mother, she silently communicated with a facial expression that she was just as surprised as he was. Vanessa's father piped up first.

"Hello young man, long time no see as they say."

Tex strolled the rest of the way into the room and stopped by his chair. With a cut from her father's eyes, Vanessa hurriedly got up and came around to hug him tightly. He returned the hug with less enthusiasm, but it came off more as if he was still in shock than rudeness.

When she returned to her seat, he forced a smile and addressed Mr. Marrow.

"Hello to you, sir. This is certainly unexpected," he said.

Ted Marrow beamed at him, leaning back and smacking a hand on T.C.'s arm with a laugh. "You can thank this one for that," he gaffed. "He finally got off his high horse and sent us an invitation. Took long enough, though."

"Apologies again, Theodore," T.C. said over his brandy. "I truly meant to do so sooner, but with business and whatnot…"

"Oh, it's fine, Conrad," Ted admonished. "If anyone understands what a burden running a business can be, it's yours truly." After sharing a grin with T.C. Ted focused on Tex and said, "Your father rang me up a few days ago and insisted we get here as soon as we could. Even used a little guilt by mentioning he thought being away from Nessa here was messing with your head."

Tex had to force himself not to glare at his father. Instead, he lifted his water and took a drink while nodding his head. When he sat the glass back down, he smiled at Vanessa and said, "Well, it has been quite a while since we've seen one another."

"Yes," she agreed cheerily.

An awkward silence followed for almost a beat too long when his mother had the sense to pipe up and ask Mrs. Marrow about whether or not her committee was ever able to secure the land for the new children's park. Realizing the hens were about to get into gossip, Ted and T.C. turned their attention to each other to discuss the various ventures they'd taken since the move. Having nowhere else to send his attention, he looked up to find Vanessa smiling at him. He returned her smile while raising his glass again.

After dinner, Tex's dad more or less told him to take Vanessa around and show her the house and grounds. His mother looked over at him, somehow able to convey that she understood what he was going through without actually showing sympathy on her face. Tex just gave her a nod to assure her that everything was alright; he was used to it. The two of them meandered through the house, with Tex pointing out various rooms, until they eventually saw all there was to see and were now sitting in the upper part of his room.

"Would you like something to drink?" he asked her, "Tea, water, soda?"

"A bottle of water will be fine," she answered.

He grabbed them both a bottle and took a seat on the other end of the couch. Vanessa let out a giggle, causing Tex to almost choke on his water. He managed not to spill it as he pulled it away and swallowed.

"What's funny?"

Her shoulders shook as her head moved slightly back and forth, and her long, glossy blond hair shimmered with the movement. Eventually, she sighed and rolled her green eyes at him with a last chuckle. "You are just cracking me up, Texas," she cooed. "You're so stiff and act like you haven't the slightest idea what to do with me."

This made Tex chuckle as well. With a shrug of his shoulders, he turned to face her fully. "Sorry about that. It's just that this is awkward, I guess. We haven't even spoken in forever, and to be completely honest," he paused, not sure exactly how to move forward, but when she leaned toward him a bit as if to indicate she was waiting for him to finish his sentence, he just blurted it out. "To be perfectly honest, I've met someone else, so I'm not really…" he stopped abruptly. This time, she was fully laughing at him. His brow furrowed.

"Oh, oh, Texas, I'm sorry," she crooned, still giggling. "I would certainly expect a guy like you to have found someone. It's not like you're ugly or backward."

He blinked twice, a little shocked that she was taking the news so well. It seems she wasn't in love with him after all, and well, that was good.

"Okay, well, that's great then," he said with relief. "I'm glad this was so easy."

She drank her water while nodding her head. "Naturally," she said, "I am going to see other people, and you are going to see other people. As long as we both understand that when all is said and done, it will be you and me at an altar during a blissfully ornate wedding ceremony, then all is right with the world."

Her sentence ended with another giggle. Tex felt a lump form in his throat, making it hard to swallow the water he was attempting to drink as he assessed her words. Was she serious or joking? He hoped she was joking, so he made sure to really bellow a laugh before he said, "Oh yes, marriage and all that. We both know that's what our parents expect."

The sudden absence of her laughter sent a chill down his neck. He looked up to find her staring at him quizzically. She cleared her throat and adjusted herself to have one leg on the couch as she put her bent arm on the top of the couch and rested her head upon it. Tex noticed she was wearing the soft, oversized sweater he had bought her for Christmas one year. His mom had picked it out. It was very light pink in color and he found himself realizing that Selena's complexion, with her darker hair and deep brown eyes, would have made the sweater much more alluring.

His attention moved back to her face as she spoke. "Tex, I wasn't joking about that," she said, her eyes squinting a little. It was like she was confused that he wasn't on the same page as her. "It's been the plan all along, and moving here hasn't changed that. I fully expect to be Mrs. Texas Conrad the Fourth someday in the very near future. I've all but been promised this by our parents and as far as I knew, you were just as on board as I am."

Tex stood up and shoved his hands in his pockets. "Are you serious right now? You are talking about an arranged marriage. We are no longer living in those antiquated days, you know, and we do not live in some third-world country."

She matched his stance, crossing her arms in front of her chest as she did. "It wouldn't be an arranged marriage, or at least I never thought of it that way," she spat vehemently, and having never seen this kind of emotion from her, it took him back a bit. "It is a marriage that makes absolute sense, and I do love you, Tex. I never would have slept with you if I hadn't. Why would you not want this?" The fact that her expression assured him she meant every word she was saying caused him to not know if he should be feeling shocked or sympathy for her ignorance. Her next words were enough to make his choice as she said, "I agree with our parents that this is a smart decision for our future and even the future of any children we may have. I thought you felt the same."

"Oh boy," Tex thought, thinking he was going to have to handle this carefully. "Um," he started, rubbing his hand on the back of his neck as he looked up for a moment. After a beat, he took a breath and held out his hands. "Vanessa, I'm not saying that I never had feelings for you. I did; you know I did, and I still care about you, but I'm in love with Selena. Like over the moon in love with her, you know?" He tugged at the bottom of his long-sleeve polo, nervously fidgeting to avoid having to make eye contact with her. "Maybe if I hadn't moved here and met her, things would be different, but this is how it is now. I mean, you said you were seeing other people too. Haven't you met anyone like that? We've both grown a lot since we were kids, Ness. Surely you can't deny that." When she hadn't responded after an awkward silence, he lifted his eyes to look at her and then wished he hadn't. Her brows were knitted together, and he could have sworn her nostrils flared just the tiniest bit.

"Texas," she began, her tone clipped and chiding, "the only thing I have done is have dates and make-out sessions. I haven't bothered opening up to anyone like that because I love you and I knew where I would end up. Who is this, Selena?"

Tex moved over to the stool at the high table and sat, unable to stop the smile from stretching across his face. "I met her on the beach when I first moved here. We've been together ever since. She is," he paused and smiled again. "There aren't words to do her justice."

"Does she come from money, like us? Is she some sort of famous supermodel or something, or has any kind of standing that's worth anything?"

"She's not like us, if that's what you mean," he growled, his face portraying the irritation he had been feeling towards everyone passing judgment on me. "Her parents have respective jobs and live well enough."

Laughter bubbled up from Vanessa's throat like a geyser spewing out hot water. Tex raised an eyebrow at her until she finally calmed down and gave him a pitying look before sauntering over to him and mewing, "Oh, Texas. You sweet, naive thing. Go ahead and have your fun with the little tart, but we both know your father will never allow you to spend your future slumming it. If his business associates thought for one second the people they were dealing with weren't up to snuff," she shook her head and sadly lifted a shoulder, "they'd quickly find a way to get out of that possible financial downfall. And what about your mother? Do you honestly think for one moment she would be able to survive and thrive if she suddenly went from this lifestyle to one of middle or even lower class?" When she reached for him, she slung an arm around his neck and peered up at him. "It will be me that you marry, and deep down you know it." She cupped the back of his head and planted a kiss on his lips before turning toward the door. "Until next time, my love," she practically sang as she walked out and closed the door behind her.

After a few minutes of fuming, Tex tried to come up with anything that would prove her wrong, and when all his decisions ultimately ended up with her being right, he snatched his keys and headed out. Stupidly, without showering first.

ten

VALENTINE'S DAY IS SUPPOSED TO BE FOR LOVE

In the weeks that followed, I was doing all I could to make myself continue in ignorant bliss, completely unaware of the fact that the surprise dinner Tex's father had arranged was just the first of many. So, Valentine's Day wasn't for love; instead, it was for waiting two hours past the expected time for your date to show up. Tex was in a foul mood, which was evident as he pushed into the living room and gave my father a curt nod before walking into the kitchen, where I was standing by the counter. He kissed me quickly before grabbing water from the refrigerator. I brought my fingers to my lips and felt them. It wasn't right, once again. There was just something about that kiss that had my mind racing and wondering.

"Did I shock you?" Tex asked me, pulling the water bottle down from his mouth. He looked extremely good in his button-up dress shirt and nice black slacks. He smelled wonderful, too. As I looked at him, I felt a twist in my gut because I really didn't want to have a bad evening with him. We'd missed so much time together because of his father. So instead of accusing him of something, I decided to just let it go.

I blinked and smiled. "No, no, I just felt a tingle."

"Are you ready to go?" he asked, then continued quickly before I could answer. "I'm sorry I'm late getting here. Father made me go through the most recent numbers from the Texacon down from the DB two times. He's now on about me putting even more of my time in with him and the board to determine the best strategies for saving our rears."

"I'm ready," I said, pulling my small black clutch from the counter, "but I don't think we'll make the movie. Do you just want to get something to eat?"

"I'm not hungry, but I'll happily take you anywhere you want to go. You look beautiful, by the way."

I looked at my dress. It was a simple red velvet short dress with a V-neck. I had red velvet heels and had taken the time to make my curls impeccable.

"Thank you," I said.

He kissed me again and then hugged me, but now even hugging me was strange. It felt, in a way, as if he were hugging me like he would never get to again. I pulled away from him.

"Do you know where you want to eat?" he asked me.

"Oh, that's alright, I don't want to go with you just sitting there watching me stuff my face."

He made an exasperated noise and frowned. "Well, what do you want to do? I'm here, aren't I? I showed up. It's Valentine's Day, and I promised you a date, which I am here to make good on."

His words were sharp. A tone and words I certainly wasn't used to and had never heard in all the time we had been together. It was his father's voice, and it was enough to make me not want to go anywhere or do anything with him at all. At first, I was hurt, and then I was angry. This must have been evident to him, as he quickly softened his features and apologized. I moved out of the kitchen, grabbed the rest of my things on the way, and went out the door.

A few seconds later, I heard Tex coming out the door and speaking to my father, promising not to have me out too late.

I tightened slightly as he slid his hands around my waist and kissed my neck. "I'm sorry, sweetheart; I'm exhausted, but it's not your fault at all. I'm trying my best to make all this work and to make everyone happy. Please forgive me."

I turned in his arms. "You don't have to try and make me happy, Tex. I love you. Just being with you, being your girl—that means everything to me. I don't demand anything from you. I'm just happy to get to love you."

He let out a long breath and hugged me close. "I know, baby, I know. You don't demand anything from me. You have no idea how much I truly appreciate that." He kissed the top of my head. "Well, enough of this. We are going to do Valentine's Day right! In true lover's fashion, my dear. So place that beautiful booty in this seat, and get ready to enjoy your night."

I smiled brightly at him and, against my better judgment, I allowed myself to just relax and truly enjoy the night. It was wonderful and, once again, he was right back to being my Tex.

We decided not to go too far since it was already so late. Just past the large mini-golf with the giant pirate looking out toward the ocean with his spyglass, there is a really nice Japanese restaurant. We were shown to the grill, where six other people who were already seated greeted us with smiles. There were four girls and three guys chatting away and laughing. I recognized the short-haired brunette with the tortoiseshell glasses. Her face was a perfect heart shape, and I'll never forget that nasally funny laugh of hers.

"Oh, hey, hey, Selena," she called while waving her skinny arm frantically. As if I could not have noticed her without the motion. I laughed a little while waving back.

"Hi, Nancy. Long time no see, huh?" I said, sitting in the seat Tex had pulled out for me.

"Very long time," Nancy replied, shoving her glasses up her face as she did. "I'll admit that I sure do miss you guys."

"We miss you, too."

Realizing I was being rude by having a conversation while my boyfriend sat clueless as to who I was talking to or why we would miss each other, I turned with a smile to introduce him, but my smile fell as I noticed he wasn't even paying attention. His thumbs were quick as whirlwinds beat along the screen of his phone.

"Tex?"

"Hmm?" he responded, not even looking up.

I placed my hand on his arm to get his attention. When he finally looked up, he noticed myself and the others watching him. Clicking the side button on his phone, he shoved it in his pants and gave his hundred-watt smile.

"Um," I said, putting the nagging feeling of wanting to know who he was texting and what was so important out of my mind. I mean, I already got pushed aside this evening for whatever reason. Couldn't he at least give me this little bit of time now? "This, uh, this is Nancy Cates. She went to school with us until freshman year before her dad took a job at the Air Force Base."

Tex stood and held out his hand to Nancy who, Lord

help us, giggled like a toddler before standing and giving her hand to him.

"It's a pleasure to meet you," Tex said, sitting back in his seat. "A friend of Selena's is a friend of mine."

"Nice to meet you, too."

The shy-looking brown-haired boy to Nancy's right cleared his throat a little more loudly than necessary. No one had to say it because we all knew that it was his way of reminding Nancy that she was his date for the evening. She wisely gave him her attention while Tex turned his attention back to me. He opened his mouth to speak, but his phone made that pinging sound that indicated he had yet another message. I know I was starting to frown, but thankfully he pulled the phone from his pocket and put it on silent. I perked back up as he grabbed my hand, brought it to his lips, and kissed my knuckles before sighing and looking me up and down.

"Have I told you how stunningly beautiful you look tonight?"

A pulse of warmth filled my face, and I knew I was blushing profusely. Even after all the firsts I'd had with this guy, he still made my stomach flutter every time he smiled at me. "You mentioned I looked nice at the house, but I'm always willing to hear it again."

"In that case," he said, then leaned into me so I could feel the slightest touch of his lips against my ear as he spoke, "allow me to reiterate. You look so incredibly sexy in that dress that I'll be hard-pressed to get through this date without tearing it off you."

Oh my. Forget blushing; I was full out on fire, and I won't even mention where the majority of the heat was building at this second. It wasn't surprising that when the chef suddenly showed up, I dropped my chopsticks and almost spilled my drink while attempting to adjust myself in my seat. Tex just chuckled knowingly, sliding his hand to my knee and giving it a squeeze. I tossed him a mischievous grin as I shook my head and rolled my eyes. He was incorrigible.

The rest of the meal was so fun. Tex and Nancy's date managed to catch the tossed shrimp in their mouths, but none of the rest of us did. The food was so good, and there were only a couple of times that Tex's private comments left me red-faced and giddy. I'm glad it wasn't any more than that, because I don't know if I could bear looking across the way and seeing Nancy waggle her eyebrows up and down one more time. I had forgotten how funny she was. After dinner, we said our goodbyes and I set up a time for her to meet up with me, Cass, and Amber. We all went to our separate vehicles with waves. They were heading to who knows where, and us... Well, let's just say I'm surprised Tex didn't get a ticket with how fast he got us to his house.

I honestly started to loosen up and just let go of any suspicions or worries I was harboring. Everything was finally getting back to normal. Tex and I were perfect once again.

Until the two nights that ended it all.

Time went on with me adjusting to seeing less of Tex, but getting one hundred percent of his attention on the occasions we could be together. Nothing but happiness and love filled my entire being as I shopped for prom dresses again with my best friends. Not once did I mention to either of them my worries or suspicions. I knew them too well. Cassey would insist we beat the secrets out of him, and Amber would suggest just "talking it out". I resigned myself to just being happy and hoping that once we graduated and Tex's father managed to fix his deals, or whatever it was Tex was always going on about, we could finally get back to us. Little did I know that T.C.'s issues had just as much to do with *my* life as they did with his.

eleven

THE NIGHT BEFORE PROM

T ex picked me up, and we went back to his house for dinner. His mother had increasingly become more solemn when I was around, and while she wasn't cruel to me and continued to smile at me and talk to me, I could tell she was holding back. It was as if she was only partly there, and she would excuse herself from us earlier and earlier.

On this particular night, she may have had a little too much to drink. She was bold and spoke harshly at the dinner table. I'll also add that it was one of the rare occasions when Mr. Conrad joined us.

"Are you going to continue to glare at me all night, Amelia?" Mr. Conrad barked at her.

"I just might, T.C.," she answered him. "What are you going to do about it? Force me to pretend to be happy by plastering an appeasing smile on my face, or pimp me out like some common hooker if it means securing your wallet."

I choked a little on my bread and had to cough twice to regain my composure. I looked across the table at Tex who was keeping his head down and his eyes on his fork, which was barely moving.

"Are you happy now, dear?" Mr. Conrad quipped. "You almost killed the gypsy."

"I'm ecstatic then, love. Won't that just solve all your problems?" she asked airily, raising an eyebrow at him and holding up her wine glass as she did.

At this point, Tex's head shot up. "Mother, please." His eyes were pleading with her. She took her furious gaze off her husband, and by the time her eyes found Tex, they looked so sad. I could feel the pity emanating from her.

"Yes, alright Texas, I'll behave, dear."

Mr. Conrad grunted. "Oh, you'll behave. That's rich, Amelia. You're going to act like you have some sense just because of the company? Let me remind you that it can be the smallest of things that can RUIN US!" He bellowed, striking a fist down onto the table for emphasis. "You've been here all year; you've listened and you've watched. You know what we're up against, and unless you want to start shopping at some discount store instead of those hoity-toity shops you find online, I suggest you fall into place!"

He jerked up from the table, causing it to clatter dishes as he did so. He moved to the door but turned around and called back.

"Texas Conrad!" he shouted out.

Tex sighed, but slowly turned his gaze to his father.

"Take care of it, son." His dad spat at him. "Do it sooner rather than later. The business, the lifestyle — it's on you, boy. I told you not to forget who you were."

With that, he stomped out of the room. Tex returned to looking at his fork. Mrs. Conrad picked up whatever drink was in her glass and began to leave the table. She stopped by me and put her hand on my face, turning my face towards her. "I am so sorry, my darling girl," she said.

I could have sworn she was going to cry, but she just took a swig of her drink and quickly left the room.

I looked over at Tex. "She didn't need to apologize." I told him, "It's not the first time I've seen your father act like a tyrant and leave the room."

A quick smirk won over Tex's face. He got up from his chair and came over to collect me from mine. "Come on. Let's go to my place."

We walked in silence to his apartment above the garage. When we were inside, he sat me on the sofa and then placed himself opposite me.

"Why do I get the feeling you are about to tell me that Santa Claus isn't real?" I asked him.

This awarded me another smirk and a couple of kisses. "I love you," he said.

"I love you too."

"Selena," he began, "you know how I've been telling you about how the Texacons here are in the red, and to get them back to the black we are going to have to merge with a partner that can put in equal equity and share in the gains and losses?"

"I remember you telling me all of that. I confess it's still a bit confusing to me as to why, because I know the Texacons are still busy and making money, but all that is none of my business."

"They are," he assured, "and the stations are still making money, but it's just not enough to cover what my father initially projected to the banks. We are running out of time for the positive to far outweigh the negative. Right now, we are about even, but come this time next year, if there isn't a monumental shift to the black, the banks are collecting regardless, which will mean goodbye to this lifestyle for us." He gestured his hand around the room, indicating the home he was in. I understood exactly what he meant.

"Oh no. I hope that doesn't happen." As I told him this, I suddenly heard his father biting out the word gypsy, and I was immediately angered, thinking that perhaps Tex was telling me all this because he was thinking I wouldn't want him if he wasn't rich. My eyebrows drew together, and I crossed my arms. "I don't love you for your money, Texas Conrad." I spat at him. "I wouldn't care if you lost every cent. You could come live with me if you needed to, or if that wouldn't do, then we could get us a cardboard box and make our mansion out of it!"

My fierce attitude caused him to chuckle, which made me even angrier.

"I'm sorry," he said while trying, and failing, to contain himself. "You're just so adorable when you're ticked off. So cute."

I swatted him, and he caught my hand. He giggled a little more, and then the seriousness returned.

"I know you aren't like that, Selena. You should know *me* as well as I know *you* by now. Whether or not you'll love me if I don't have a swollen bank account doesn't worry me at all."

"Then what is worrying you?" I asked him, finally showing the fright I was feeling and had been feeling for months.

His voice caught a little as he tried to answer. He took a moment, cleared his throat, and tried again. "What's worrying me is whether or not you'll love me when you truly know what is expected of me as a member of this family, as the heir to Texacon."

He wouldn't look at me, but he kept my hand in his and brought it up to his lips. He kissed my fingers with a deep sigh.

"Tex, you're scaring me a little," I said softly. "Please tell me what is going on."

He stood up and paced back and forth. I just watched him. I watched him, knowing he was trying to gain courage. He was digging deep within himself and fighting because every part of him was trying *not* to tell me something, while every other part of him was trying *to* tell me. As long as he could remember, life had been like this. Him having to weigh his wants and dreams against the will of his dad. Tex was grinding his teeth while acknowledging that it never gets any easier.

I licked my lips and sat up. "There's someone else, isn't there?" I asked, a tear rolling down my face.

His eyes closed, and his voice hitched. "Yes," he admitted, "but it's not what you think. Not in that sense anyway."

I barked out a laugh. "Not what I think? Isn't that exactly what I think? The man I love has been keeping something from me or hasn't been faithful to me. Is there *any way* that can be an okay statement?"

My tears went from a light trickle to a downpour in mere seconds.

He turned to me, his hands out and pleading. "It's so much more complicated than that. You haven't been brought up like I have — my father, my family. I haven't been completely honest with you, but you don't even know…"

But I didn't let him finish. "I don't know. *I* don't know?" I was mockingly laughing and had my hand turned back into my chest as I bellowed at him. "I know, Tex, I KNOW! Let me assure you that I *know* that when I kiss your lips, more often than not, I can tell something just isn't right. I *know* that when you hug me or pull me close, you will sometimes hold onto me so tightly that I feel as if you are making it the last time you ever do so. I know Tex; I have known!" I started to lose it. I was crumbling and dying. "I just… didn't want to BELIEVE!"

I finished my speech with a shuttering gasp. The ache I had been holding back for months was allowed to rip me open.

Tex watched in horror. His hand came up to his mouth as his own eyes spilled tears. "Selena, please, let me explain," he begged, "please let me just tell you everything before you think the absolute worst."

I couldn't speak, even if I wanted to. I jerked tissues from the box on the table and held them to my face. I felt the sofa sink beside me, then saw Tex hunched over with his head in his hands. He swallowed twice before speaking quietly and softly.

"Right after this year's homecoming," he began, "my father took me into his office and showed me just how close we are to losing everything. I asked him what he expected me to do about it. I haven't even graduated from school yet."

Tex got up to pace again; it seemed he couldn't sit and talk.

"Well," he continued, "he told me he was glad I asked because he was going to tell me exactly what I was going to do about it." He paused, staring at me. He was breathing hard, and I could tell he could lose it at any second as well.

I wiped my face. "And…" I urged.

"There is a very wealthy businessman by the name of Tommy Ewing. He has successful businesses in the tri-state area. He has a few restaurants and a couple of convenience stores. Word got out that he was looking to get into oil and gas. My father picked up on this news and arranged a meeting. If everything goes the way Father wants, then we'll not only get out of the slump we are currently in, we will also stand to triple our net worth."

"Okay, well, that's a good thing, right?" I was confused as to what this had to do with him being unfaithful or any other problem.

"Yes," Tex agreed, stopping to look at me.

I looked at him once and then dropped my eyes. He moved again and struck his fist against his leg.

"Father demands that Mother and I uphold an expected image," he added reluctantly. "He told me I was to make sure the public only sees me as a well-rounded and well-bred Texas gentleman. I am to be the picture of what any wealthy, white American male should be. Privileged, entitled, and selective to guarantee there is nothing that could interfere with our way of life."

"So," I began, "let me see if I am understanding this. Since around October of last year, you have been spending so much time away from me, away from all of us, just so this Ewing guy doesn't find out that your girlfriend is of gypsy descent and one of your best friends is black?"

"I…" Tex started and then closed his mouth briefly. He finally answered after a moment. "In a nutshell, yes, but that isn't the worst of it."

I nodded my head. "And what would that be?" I asked, as a fresh wave of tears streamed from my eyes. I felt my chest tighten as my insides began to twist, not wanting to acknowledge it but, deep down, knowing what he was about to say.

"I had a girlfriend of sorts before I moved here. She is exactly the kind of girl my father expects me to end up with. I had thought I left her in the past when we moved, but Father has lived up to expectations. She's been coming around for a while now." He answered, dropping his head and rubbing his neck.

Can I possibly explain to you the feeling of complete and total collapse? If I can't get you to imagine the hollowing out of your very heart, then let me at least tell you when you can expect to know this pain for yourself. It's the exact moment—the very precise moment — when the one you love tells you forthright that there is a possibility that they will be ending your relationship, maybe even going so far as to act as if said relationship never happened in the first place.

I was numb, but I could move. I typed in my phone for a car and gave them the address of the convenience store about two blocks from where I was.

"What are you doing?" Tex asked me, noticing my finished text.

I gathered my things and slowly made my way off the couch. He moved in front of me quickly, grabbing my arms in his hands.

"Selena, what are you doing? Where are you going?" he asked me.

"Please…" I answered back. It was all I could manage. "Please."

He gazed at me, his eyes searching my face. I'm sure he knew I was gone, already in a heap inside myself. He grabbed his keys.

"No, no," I protested, "I'm covered. I'm just going to go."

"No, Selena, don't do this. I don't want you to go! I love you, and I want you always. Just sit down and talk to me," he pleaded.

"I can't do this. I can't even think clearly at the moment."

I was at the door now.

In a flash he was beside me, crying just as I was.

He placed his head on mine and swallowed. "Please don't leave me. We can figure this out. I should have involved you a long time ago; I should have confided in you. I didn't know what to do, and I still don't. I'm stuck. My father keeps using my mother as guilt over my head and my responsibility to the family. I'm scared, Selena, and most of all I'm terrified of losing you! I told you now; I'm telling you now because I know you're not stupid, and you know something just isn't right… Please talk to me."

I took a shuddering breath and said, "I just can't right now."

"Alright then, alright. I understand. I do. You need to think; I need to think, because I'm still so lost." He was blabbering now.

I turned the knob. He caught my hand. "Prom babe. It's prom tomorrow. I will be there to pick you up. Please be ready, okay? I'll pick you up, and we'll go to prom, and then we'll come back here and we'll figure this out. I need you, Selena."

I left by agreeing to prom, and he followed me because he refused to let me walk by myself in the dark. When I reached the lighted parking lot, I turned and waved him away. He stopped but didn't leave until I was in the car and heading out of sight.

When I got home, I rushed straight to my bathroom, closed and locked the door, and then allowed every ripped shred of my soul to cry out into a towel. If I hadn't muffled my sobs, I know someone would have called the police over a possible murder taking place. I cried hard and long. I don't think I ever stopped, because when I woke up on the bathroom floor the next morning, tears were still streaming down my face.

PROM NIGHT

T ex had been blowing up my phone all morning. It wasn't until the afternoon that I answered his call and told him I was getting ready and that, yes, we were still going. I called the girls and told them that Tex and I would be going in his car. They seemed disappointed, but I told them it was because we would be running a little late due to Tex's work with his dad, and we just didn't want them to have to wait. The truth is… I just couldn't fathom the idea of trying to act like everything was okay when it most definitely wasn't.

I did my hair and makeup and then took a long breath before sliding into my dress. I loved this dress. It was one of a kind. I had gone to three different stores, and just when I was about to double back and settle for a navy blue strapless dress, I saw the perfect light shade of pale yellow peeking out of a rack. The dress was shoved in tight with tons of others that had been pulled from old inventory. I tried it on and knew it was the one. The chiffon was light, and the fit was perfect. The top was a halter that had additional off-the-shoulder sleeve strips. It was snug and trimmed to my waist, and the bottom was cut up high on my right thigh and then angled while flowing out to the ground. It was beautiful.

I approved of my reflection before going downstairs to be bombarded by my parents and their desire to take a million pictures.

We were supposed to be there at six. When he wasn't at my house by five, I started calling and texting. When I didn't get a response back, I told my parents I was going to meet him at his place because he had gotten stuck doing something for his dad and was just now getting ready. They said alright, that they understood, and to make sure we came back after the dance so they could get pictures of us together. I assured them we would.

I know it is *super bad* to lie to your parents, but what would you have done? Said, "Oh, hey, Mom and Dad, you know my boyfriend... Well, he's sort of maybe breaking up with me, but don't worry, it's just complicated and so what and so on."

Well, no thank you to that nightmare. With a smile at the door, I drove out of the driveway and headed to Tex's house.

There is this feeling for people like me; perhaps, you have felt this too. I've been told by my mother that it is the gypsy in us — our gut intuition, if you will. Regardless of what it is, I just know it stinks, big time. The best way to describe it is to think of your stomach and where it is. It's not something we put a lot of thought into on a regular basis, right? Now, just imagine how you think it would feel inside if, all of a sudden, your stomach just dropped down to your intestines. Can you imagine that? Have you felt something like that before? Because that is exactly what was happening to me right at that moment. I was driving, already crying even though I had no idea what was going on, and in an instant, my stomach dropped, and I knew my whole world was about to completely fall apart.

I came to the driveway and noticed a sleek, sporty silver car close to the garage. I could have driven past it; the wrap-around drive was huge, but I decided to make a U-turn and come back to enter from the other side. I whipped the car around so that I was facing back out of the entrance. I don't know why, but I just knew I had to do this. I got out of the car and had to walk across the driveway to the porch, then turn to get to the steps leading up to Tex's room. I climbed the stairs, wondering what I was going to say or trying to think of any plausible explanations for why he would have stood me up. Maybe he was just so tired he fell asleep, or maybe he was in the main house still with his father, and T.C. wouldn't let him leave. All these perfectly innocent scenarios were dancing in my thoughts while my heart was scolding me with each beat. Every two thumps telling me *You know (da dum) You know (da dum) You know (da dum)*...

When I reached the door, I started to knock, but I didn't. I let my hand fall because I was drawn instead to the large window around the side. The one above the garage door that Tex and I would stare out of as we lay in his bed together. I would look up at the stars and ask him what constellations were up there, and was that the big dipper or the little dipper? My heart fluttered, and I slowly stepped from the door to the window.

I looked down into his room. I looked with love at the young man who completed me and made me ecstatic to live my life. The same young man was now killing me, body and soul. My eyes flooded and ran over, and my chest heaved as I watched a beautiful blond girl button up her blouse before strapping on her heels. I crumbled as she grabbed her purse and made her way to Tex, kissing him deeply before turning to go. My stomach settled firmly against my intestines as Tex shoved on the pants for his prom tux and tried to dress quickly. He grabbed his watch and checked it. Then, realizing something horrifying, he checked it again. His body turned quickly to snatch his phone. Another burst of realization hit him when he saw the time and how many calls and texts he had missed from me. He looked up and shouted the *F* word, but in doing so, he locked eyes with me. There was not a sound in the world except for the small sob that escaped my throat.

I bolted, and honey, I mean I *BOLTED*! There aren't words that could describe how I managed to get from where I was, down the stairs, and halfway across the porch before Tex could even make it out the door.

"SELENA!" I heard him roar out into the night, "SELENA WAIT! SELENA!"

I went to run down the porch stairs. I heard the front door opening just as my shoe caught in the bottom of my flowing dress. I fell hard. An instant later, his mother was beside me, helping me. She was crying herself and mewling at me.

"Oh dear, oh sweet girl," she was saying.

I hiked the dress up into my hands and shot like a bullet for my car. I was in it and turning the key when Tex had just made it to the front door, still screaming after me. I never looked into the rearview mirror. I never looked back.

I didn't see Tex's father shoot out of the door and wrap his son in his arms, keeping him from coming any closer to me. I didn't hear his father shout at him to let me go—that it was over and it was for the best. I didn't see Tex fight with his father until he was wrestled to the ground and held there. I didn't know that, eventually, Tex would sneak off in his car and race to my home. I never heard him beg my parents about where I was or if they had seen me. Neither

Amber nor Cassey knew what to do when Tex showed up at the prom like a raging lunatic trying to find me and ended up slinging Patty's hands off him and telling her to buy some panties and wear them for heaven's sake. Lastly, I wasn't aware of the worry and fear I caused my parents and my friends because I didn't go to prom and I didn't go home. I died, and then I drove for two hours.

thirteen

THE COST OF COWARDICE

Tex had been driving around for almost four hours when he turned into the boardwalk parking lot and got out of the car. He had been to the dance, to my parent's house, to the Dairy Barn, and anywhere else he could think I might have gone. This was his last resort. The beach where they'd first met—the place that started it all.

The lights on the boardwalk were at full power as he walked toward that enormous statue of Poseidon with the dolphins jumping around him. That's how he'd come upon me that day. He'd been just about everywhere on this beach since mid-morning and had finally gotten around to wanting to examine the statue when, just down from it, I'd lay stretched out looking glorious in that black bikini. A smile tugged his lip up his cheek at the memory and how badly he wanted to talk to me just from that first look.

On his left side were all manner of souvenir shops selling everything from hermit crabs to clothes and beach gear. Neon lights shone out from sandy glass windows, and laughter from kids running and chasing each other would tinkle through the air as he passed families that were either on their way back to their vehicles after a long day of fun and sun or diving into a burger joint where they would get a quick hot meal or some type of treat. To his right, the stars shone high above him, unburdened by a cloudless sky. The moon was so full and bright that a halo glowed around it. Tex's steps went from thunks on wood to soft swifts of sand as he stepped off onto the beach in the direction of the statue.

A prom tux was not the best attire to be wearing when slumping through sand, but he was grateful for the vest and jacket as a chilled wind snaked through his hair and blew it from his face. He rubbed at that face before massaging his neck, already feeling the beginnings of a five-o'clock shadow. Did stress make beards grow faster?

The statue was only a few steps away when his heart bottomed out. The sliver of hope he'd been holding onto that I would have come here faded like the entrails of a freshly blown-out candle flame. He sat heavily on the stone base and dropped his head in his hands. It didn't take long for the sobs to begin. I was gone, and he knew it wasn't just for the evening or until I had calmed down, but gone for good. He'd lost me completely because he had been too much of a coward to fight for what he wanted. There was no good explanation for what he'd done—none! Even if his father had done all he could to keep us apart, Tex still didn't have to carry on with Vanessa the way he had, but he convinced himself that he needed Vanessa and that what he was doing was to keep her happy so she and his father would let him be. She was just a means to an end.

An unconvinced snort was replaced by a sob as he scolded himself. The truth was that he didn't think he'd get caught and would be able to spend as much time with me as he could. A small part of him had even devised a plan to get in touch with a prominent college that would have me moving away from here to get my degree. That way he could go to me wherever I was, and I'd be none the wiser. He knew it was that whole *"have your cake and eat it too"* scenario, but there was no way on earth he could ever bring himself to let me go. It seemed like a good plan but then, after Vanessa got spooked because she realized Tex wasn't exactly on the same page as her, she had made it a point to come around more and more frequently.

With a long and heavy sigh, Tex leaned back against Poseidon's legs and blinked out the last dregs of tears. No more, he thought, no more living this way. It cost him everything, and he was not going to spend the rest of his life in misery. He allowed himself a few more precious moments to mourn before hauling himself up and stomping back to his car with determination. Another plan was already forming in his mind. The first thing he would have to do was get his father off his back by securing a business deal. After that, he would tell his father exactly how his life will be from now on, whether he liked it or not. Once all that was taken care of, he would have to inform Vanessa that they were completely done and would never be together again under any circumstances, and lastly, he was going to atone for what he'd done to me. Every moment from here on out would be spent finding any way that he could to do right by me and hoping and praying that God would see fit to send me back to him one day.

The first part of the plan went better than expected. He was able to see Mr. Ewing the next day. Tex entered the extravagantly decorated office of Jackson Ewing and was offered a seat in one of the shining leather and wood chairs, just a foot from the carved mahogany desk. Rather than a nameplate that sat atop it, there was a plaque attached boldly to its front with Jackson A. Ewing in beautiful calligraphy scripted across it. Tex declined the seat as his nerves were too on edge to sit still properly.

Mr. Ewing's brows knitted together as he took in the sight of Tex before him. It was evident the boy was troubled, and a protective fatherly concern straightened his spine. He wasn't young by any means. Seventy-seven years and thin silver hair were at the forefront of his appearance, not to mention a slight bow of the back from osteoporosis and a slower gait when he walked. But his mind was still sharp, and those piercing blue eyes never missed a thing. When Tex asked that he please listen to him, Ewing indicated for him to speak by gesturing with his hand and slowly settling himself into the soft brown chair behind him.

"Mr. Ewing, I know you are looking to create a merger with my father and get into oil and gas. If you haven't heard already, my father is more than eager to seal this deal with you. I am here today because he believes that certain aspects of our lives could make a difference in whether or not you are willing to do business with us." Tex paused to shove one hand in his pocket as the other pinched the bridge of his nose. He had to get these next words right. Everything else depended on exactly how things were going right now. "What I'm trying to say, sir, is that I don't believe in setting a standard by which I am to live in order to be accepted by a certain ideal of people. I know a lot of wealthy people, our kind of people, have certain expectations for how we are to behave and the company we keep." Tex finally made eye contact as he clasped his hands behind his back and puffed his blue-sweatered chest out in confidence. "What it comes down to is that I am in love with a young lady who is not rich, who is not like us, and whose family comes from a long line of gypsies," he laughed a little, "famous gypsies apparently." He cleared his throat, moving his hands to touch the edge of the desk as he finished his speech. "Regardless, the point is that if my being in love with someone like Selena is enough to keep you from wanting to enter into a business agreement with my family, then I'm sorry to say that you are not the type of person we need to be doing business with anyway."

The room was silent as Jackson took stock of the young man before him. Every bit of the boy was a younger version of the ruthless tycoon he'd been dealing with for the past couple of months, but he could tell upon further inspection that Tex was going to be even more successful. Not just because of the way he carried himself, but because of all he'd laid before him today. A sly smile slid up his face as he held up a finger for Tex to hold on for just a minute while he slid the desk drawer open to his right. His frail fingers trembled just the slightest as he lifted the picture book out and opened the front cover. Tex's face twisted in confusion as he took in the sight of the photos being flipped before him. He matched Jackson's smile with one of his own.

TIME TO HEAL

So, while it is true that my great-great grandfather was the legendary James Edgar Ayers, and I played that off a bit since Tex's father had a revulsion to that fact, it's my grandmother that embraces our gypsy heritage the most. My mother always said I would never be able to get anything past Grandma Pearl's "gypsy eye". This would explain why she was already standing on her porch, arms crossed, and nodding her head as she watched me pull the car up and park. I got out and trudged my way up the walk to stand before her. Even though I was in emotional pain, the sight of Grandma's familiar soft yellow two-story house with the wrap-around porch was comforting to me. The peach trees, especially the overly large one in the front yard with my old tire swing still hanging, were a true sight for sore eyes. I breathed in the familiar scent of the blooming flowers as I trudged up to stand before her.

"I've made up your room," she told me, "you'll have to call your mom and dad; they are in a fit wondering where you are."

I looked up at her face; fresh tears ran down my cheeks,

and my shoulders shuddered. Grandma Pearl sighed. Her skirt swished as she made her way down the steps to me and placed an arm around me, guiding me up the steps and speaking as she did.

"You are going to go inside now and cry to your heart's content. I have chocolate and lots of warm blankets. You will stay with me now. Time heals all wounds."

My response was a whimper, but I did just as she said.

In the weeks that followed, I called my mom and broke down everything with her. We cried together, and she told me to come home. I just couldn't. I couldn't be anywhere that he was. I also called Amber and Cassey and told them everything. They told me how Tex had and was still constantly calling them or coming to find them and asking if they'd heard from me.

"Now that I know all this," Cassey growled, "you just wait until I see or talk to him again. Just wait. How dare he…"

"No, Cass," I told her, "don't do or say anything, please. It's not necessary."

"NOT NECESSARY!" she shouted. "Not necessary? It is very necessary. He's not getting away with this. Tossing you to the curb after he got his fill and claiming he '*has to*' for the benefit of his family. Acting like he just had to sleep with that skank and had no choice. It's all horse hock, Selena, and you know it!"

"Cassey, calm down!" Amber scolded.

They were both at Amber's house and had me on speaker. I could feel Cassey rolling her eyes and crossing her arms in front of her chest while Amber gave her a look and silently pleaded with her to think about my feelings.

"Selena," Amber began, "listen, hon, we haven't told Tex a thing about where you are or what we've talked to you about. We told him that, of course, we've talked to you;

we're your best friends, but we also told him that all you've said is that you two are over and you need to get away to heal. He still tries to get us to tell you things or send you things. I think he also tries to get information from your parents as well, but no one is giving him anything."

"Thank you, guys. I appreciate it; I do." I told them.

"Are you coming back soon?" Amber asked me.

There was silence for a while, and then I took a breath and told them what I had known all along. "No, I won't be coming back soon. I won't be coming back at all."

"What?" they exclaimed. "What about graduation? Our senior trip? What about us, Selena? You aren't going to just abandon us too are you?"

"I'll never abandon you guys, and you know it. I'm finishing school with homeschooling and staying here with Grandma Pearl. I can't be there. I know you guys understand that. As for the senior trip, I'll still go with you all as long as Tex doesn't try to pal along with Derek and Pete."

There was a snort on their end of the line. "Derek won't be coming either. I am so over his crap!" Cassey said.

There was another pause, and then Amber and I laughed together.

"I'm serious this time!" Cassey demanded.

This made us laugh that much harder, and she finally joined in. When the call ended, we had told each other how much we loved one another and promised to text, Face-Time, and call. I wouldn't desert my friends, and I knew they wouldn't desert me.

Time moved on, and eventually, Tex stopped bothering my family and friends. They assured me they hadn't heard from him since graduation. I would have been content to settle with the phrase *"out of sight, out of mind"* but fate is cruel and loves to extend your misery whenever she can. The news about two major business tycoons merging companies and expanding into Dallas, Texas, was every-where. T.C. had gotten exactly what he wanted. A compliant son and to, once again, be king of the world. Well, of the state of Texas anyway.

It seemed like I would never be able to function again. The only way I could cope with existing at all was to pretend it never happened. It was not easy, but it was possible. The more time that went on, the easier it got. By September, I had signed up for my first year of college. My friends and I stayed close. Amber and Pete got married in Hawaii. It was a beautiful wedding. No one mentioned Tex at all. Cassey and Derek got an apartment together while they attended community college. Last year, he moved out. Two days ago, he moved back in. They haven't changed.

As the college years passed, my misery subsided and my laughter returned. I had some dates, but nothing serious. I just couldn't allow that. Grandma Pearl told me that it takes longer for the hardened shell to crack on a time-healed heart, but that it would eventually crack and shed altogether.

I don't remember the exact painful feelings I had; I just know I had them. I don't remember how long I cried and mourned, but I know I did. What I know more than anything is that those are two things I never wanted to experience again, so if it's all the same for Grandma Pearl, I'll just keep that hardened shell right around my heart, all safe and secure.

part two

SOME YEARS LATER

fifteen

NOT COMPLETELY HEALED, BUT AT LEAST SCABBED OVER

After my mother begged me day in and day out for months, I finally caved and told her I would come back home. It's time, I believe, and Grandma Pearl keeps telling me I'm what is causing her to not get any dates anymore. She says the men think she's still raising children, so they won't ask her out. How could I let my grandma keep suffering the pangs of being single? She's only seventy years old, after all.

We both knew and felt it was time. The night before I left, Grandma Pearl sat me down at the kitchen table and took my hands in hers. She told me to remain strong and always trust my intuition. She told me our ability to just know and feel is a gift from God, passed down from gypsy mother to gypsy daughter. It's a special gift. I hugged her tight and told her how much I loved her. She was smiling and waving as I drove away and headed back to Saint Caine.

I had spent the past few years with my parents coming out to Grandma Pearl's on my birthdays, Christmas, and all other special occasions. I hadn't laid eyes on my own home for what seemed like forever. I expected so much to be different, but it wasn't. The wood was still chocolate brown. The front door was still cream-colored, with a little window at the top. I knew around the back would be a fenced-in yard, and a deck Dad had built extended out to the middle of it. Home. I was home.

Mom rushed out and ran to the car before I had even fully stopped. The woman acted like she hadn't seen me at all, but I guess that was to be expected. She had told me time and time again how she hated passing my room, knowing I wasn't there and wouldn't be for a while. I thought this meant that my room would be the same as when I left, but thankfully it wasn't. Mom had remodeled the room to accommodate a *"more adult me"* as she put it. I was grateful. When I left, Tex was everywhere in this room along with every memory of him. Now the room was a different color and had a different feel. I admired the soft tan of the walls, accented by the cream-colored molding wrapping around the top. Not a thing was the same, except for my gigantic dollhouse, and the only pictures in the room were the tall paintings of a boy and a girl in carnival costumes. The wicker furniture had been replaced with softwood. A matching set between the bed, chest of drawers, nightstand, and vanity. Mom gave me a one-arm squeeze as we looked over the room, and then she helped me get settled in.

I had expected to feel like a fish out of water, but it was no time at all before I was back into old routines and habits. Even though Cass had her apartment now, we still gathered at her parent's house for bonfires on the beach. At least three nights a week we were having mini-reunions at the DB, and apart from game night being at Amber and Pete's own house instead of at either of their parents' houses, we were still squabbling like school kids over who was cheating. I didn't realize how much I had missed living with my parents. It was beyond nice to come down to breakfast with them at the table and to sit in between them on the couch in the living room.

Life had settled, and I was functioning well when I landed my dream job.

I was extremely nervous going in for the interview. I had completed my degree in journalism, and this would be a big break for me to get to write. Not fluff pieces either, like I'd been writing for the university paper and submitting to online magazines. This was going to be actual journalistic writing. Three times, I typed up my resume. I was on my fifth draft, arranging my portfolio and taking out things that I didn't feel truly showed my potential. I knew I had an innate ability to grasp a story and make the reader feel as if they were right there, living it, seeing it, and hearing it. Mom eventually snatched the portfolio case from my hands, zipped it, and said, "*Enough*". She gave me her best mom's glare too, so I couldn't argue. I may be twenty-five years old, but she's still my mom!

The building where the Saint Caine Syndicate was born and released was off the north end of the interstate. If you left the DB parking lot, you would turn right and drive for about seven miles before the mammoth brick structure loomed out at you. Having a job that was around a twenty-minute drive from home would be another perk.

Inside, the building splits into two functioning businesses. You have the Syndicate, which you get to by entering the building and taking a winding flight of stairs to the left of the reception desk. The other business is the law firm Laughlin, Harmon, and James which, as I'm sure you've guessed, you would take to the right side of reception and follow the winding stairs. The building houses elevators as well since it's six stories in total, but most people working on the second floor usually take the stairs.

The moment I made my way through the rotating doors, I inhaled the smell of fresh paper and a clean, crisp office. My heels clicked on the floor as I made my way to the reception desk. The girl behind the counter looked about my age. To my horror, I realized she was exactly my age as I moved closer and closer. She was talking on the phone. It was one of those headpieces that allowed you to listen and speak without having to hold onto anything.

"Yes," she was saying, "I told him that it was either the house or the car. I didn't care which one I got, but it better be one or the other."

After this statement, she blew on her freshly filed nail as she rolled her eyes to see me walking right up to her.

"Oh, my dang," she drew out each word before gaffing a laugh. "Tabs, you are not going to freaking believe this! Selena 'goody-two-shoes' Ayers has just sauntered up to my desk!" She laughed aloud again, sweeping her hair off her shoulders as she did. "No. I swear it, Tabs, she is right in front of me!"

"And she can hear you," I said, smiling and tilting my head at her. I could also hear Tabitha on the phone mic jutting out of Patty's hair, but I didn't care to mention it.

"Selena Ayers, as I live and breathe, how long has it been?" she asked me.

I let out a breath. "Patty Kearns. How nice to see you, too. It's been almost seven years."

Patty sat up against the desk and folded her arms atop it. I had thought she would hang up with Tabitha, but clearly, she wanted to let "Tabs" in on our conversation.

"It's Kearns-Harmon now," she mewed, flinging a

heavily jeweled left hand at the sign above her head. She let the hand rest in front of me and flicked her ring finger just to make sure I noticed the insanely large diamond.

"Did she see the ring?" I heard Tabitha ask from the phone mic.

I leaned forward a little bit. "She sees it, Tabs," I sang out sweetly, "don't think I could miss it from space, hon."

One of Patty's eyebrows shot up briefly as her smile widened. She was enjoying rubbing her financial good fortune in my face. If only she knew how much I just didn't care. Oh well, I had other important things to do.

"I have an appointment with Mr. Darnell," I told Patty.

"Uh-huh," she murmured, making a show of straightening up and tapping away on the computer keys.

"Yes, you do," she confirmed. "Applying for the mail room?" she asked next, not even trying to hide the mocking laugh of an undertone.

I laughed back in the same fashion. "No, silly," I told her, letting my right-hand flap out at her because she was just too funny. "I'm applying for the journalist position. We can't all marry lawyers and just hang around and look pretty. Some of us have intelligence and earn degrees to make a living, so we don't have to collect alimony when our rich husbands leave us for their secretaries once we're old and wrinkled." I batted my lashes at her.

All the humor washed from her face in an instant. I heard Tabitha's gasp and snort before her comment, "Oh, no, she didn't."

Patty's finger slammed into a button on her station while her face gave me the most hateful look she could muster.

"Reception!" she barked into the new line. "I have a *Ms.* Ayers in the lobby for Mr. Darnell."

I took notice of how she inflected the *s* in Ms. It seems

she also thought that being single bothered me as well. It's to be expected. She didn't know me in school, and wasn't going to know me now.

"Yes. Thank you."

She slammed the button again and then closed her hand over the microphone endpiece. "Go up the stairs, make a left, walk to the end of the hall, and turn right. Mrs. Wynley will take care of you from there."

She spun her chair around so her back was facing me. I sang out a "thank you" as I moved away from the desk and to the stairs. She had never hung up with Tabitha, and just as I was reaching the bottom step, I heard her bite out, "As if I care, everyone knows she went bat crap crazy after Texas Conrad tossed her aside."

I let her conversation fade away from me. A few years ago, I might have been frozen in place by that remark. I would have been too infuriated to move, too enraged to even contemplate placing one foot in front of the other. Now... I was able to take in that comment, breathe through it, and continue.

I made my way to the top of the stairs and was just beginning to take the left turn when I was bumped and almost knocked off my feet. My portfolio burst open, and more than half of my work went sliding onto the polished floor. I made a disgusted noise and immediately went to try to piece together my work once more. Strong hands were in my line of vision, moving equally fast to try and gather my things. The problem with that was that this person was mixing up the dated material.

"I've got it!" I spat.

"I'm truly sorry. I had my back turned and didn't see you." A male voice explained.

"It's fine!" I growled.

"No, it's not. I shouldn't have been backing up really, but I'm having the new name signs put up above our office and was trying to make sure they were even or centered. Well, correct, I guess is the right word."

To be honest, I wasn't even listening to his babbling. I was so incensed over my papers that I just snatched them out of his hand, shoved them into my case, and finally looked at him while saying, "What are you going on about?" in my most irritated voice.

This was also the time when I looked at the man trying to help me to my feet. I quickly closed my mouth. He continued to help me rise while readjusting my purse on my arm. I skimmed my hand up the strap to help.

He laughed nervously, rubbing his hand behind his head and squinting a bit. He looked back at the far-right side of the dividing balcony, and I saw where workers on ladders were trying to adjust large gold letters above the spaced-out glass doorways. He extended the hand that had been rubbing his head and used it to indicate the sign hanging I hadn't noticed before.

"The sign," he admitted sheepishly, "I was trying to back up and get the whole view. So to speak." His shoulders moved up and down, and he sighed out a breath before extending his hand to me. "Ryan James," he said.

I looked once more at the sign, noticing the name James at the end of it, and looked back at him. I extended my hand and took his. "Selena Ayers," I told him, then pulled my hand back. "I accept the apology and thank you for helping gather my things."

I pulled my portfolio into my arms, moved around the banister, and made my way to the hall that would lead to Mr. Darnell's office. I was stopped abruptly as Mr. James moved in front of my path.

"It's nice to meet you, Selena," he said, smiling and bending his head a little to make eye contact with me. I held his stare and lifted an eyebrow. "Let me, um…" he stumbled. "Let me make it up to you. Running into you, I mean."

"That's not necessary; thank you," I said shortly, moving to go around him.

He moved with me once more. "I insist," he said. "It's the least I can do. I mean, it's possible I ruined your pieces, and it seems you are heading to the Syndicate for an interview, I presume?" He squinted those eyes again. I noticed them for the first time. They were a light hazel color. The kind of color that will change depending on the color of the clothes he wears. Like, if he wears a blue shirt, then his eyes will take on more of a bluish hue, but if the shirt is green, then they will seem greener. I took in the rest of his features. He was clean-shaven with dark hair. I thought he might be Latino. He was about three inches taller than me, so I had to look up at him. I must have been staring, because he laughed a little and looked down shyly. I shook my head to get it together.

"Look," I said, "I need to get down this hallway. It is bad enough that perhaps some of my pieces are ruined; however, it will be a no-go if I show up late on top of it. So, if you don't mind, would you kindly, please, move out of my way so I can at least get something right today?"

He held his hands up in mock surrender and reluctantly moved aside. "I understand."

"Thank you."

"You're quite welcome."

"Ok, I appreciate it. Goodbye now." I was moving down the hall. He had moved behind me and was just standing there, calling to me as I walked.

"You said your name was Selena?"

"Yes," I called back, pushing my hair behind my ear but still moving forward.

"Selena... Ayers, was it?"

"Yes!" I called back again, exasperated this time.

"Alright then. Good luck, Selena Ayers."

I rolled my eyes and huffed just as I reached the door to Mr. Darnell's office. "Thanks again!" I shot out but didn't turn or look at him as I spoke. Two seconds later, I was standing in front of Mrs. Wynley and all thoughts of Ryan James were now gone from my consciousness.

Thankfully, I made it to the interview on time. This didn't stop Mr. Darnell from making me wait another half hour in the lobby while he took an important phone call, but I didn't mind as long as he knew I was on time. While I waited, I used the opportunity to fix all the problems with my now-scrambled portfolio. I was adjusting the last page when Mrs. Wynley informed me that, "Mr. Darnell will see you now."

I smiled at her; she was super sweet. Her voice was a little high-pitched, and she reminded me of a Disney fairy godmother. She was a little on the heavy side because she liked sugary treats and baked goods, but that didn't stop her from enjoying life and smiling brightly every chance she got. She gave me a return smile and drew her shoulders in. "Good luck, dear," she told me.

I thanked her and made my way into Mr. Darnell's office.

Almost an hour later, I was shaking Mr. Darnell's hand and thanking him so much for the opportunity. I assured him three more times that he wouldn't be disappointed, then finally got myself out of there and back out into the hallway. I ignored Patty K. on my victory stroll out to the exit and was just about to push my way out the doors when my name was called.

"Selena Ayers."

I stopped abruptly and turned to see Ryan James quickly taking the last of the stairs and making his way to me. I made a face, certainly confused as to what he would want with me. We already had a few awkward minutes, wasn't that enough? He was either nervous or out of breath when he caught up to me at the door. Behind him, I could see Patty staring us down and firing up her headset. She was probably calling Tabitha again. I focused on Ryan in front of me.

"Yes?" I asked.

He ran a hand through his hair and fidgeted with his tie. "Um, wow," he muttered. "I was all set with words before, but now it seems they've abandoned me."

"I'm sorry?" I said, leaning in to try and understand him.

He smiled at me, then took a deep breath before saying, "Listen, uh... I know you were here for an interview and all, not to get hit on, but it just so happens that this is where I've run into you." He paused before adding, "Literally!" with a smirk.

I smiled, despite myself. He was very cute. "I told you it's fine. I'm okay, no harm done, and I still managed to get the job."

"That's great!" he said, smiling brightly. "Then you have a reason to celebrate."

"I guess so," I said, shrugging my shoulders.

"So you'll allow me to take you to dinner."

"You want to take me out?" I asked him.

"Well, yes. I feel I owe you for possibly causing you to almost not get the job."

"But I did get the job." I interrupted, smiling as I did.

"Right," he added. "So then, there is a better reason. I take you to dinner to make up for running into you, *and* I take you to dinner to celebrate your success today. It's a win either way. You get dinner."

"Uh-huh," I said curiously, "and what's the purpose of all of this for you? A clear conscience? I told you I got the job, so no harm was done."

"I would have thought that was obvious," he said softly, "my purpose is to spend time with you."

I paused, narrowing my eyes as a flutter flitted through my chest. "You don't even know me."

"Yes, but I want to."

There was silence for a beat. For the first time in almost a decade, I felt it again. The little bumps erupted on my arms, and the hair stood up on my neck. I knew from the heat on my cheeks that I had blushed. I dropped my eyes for a moment to smile and then looked back up at him.

"Alright," I told him.

He motioned out the door, and I let him lead me to my car. We talked a little, enough for me to tell him where I lived and when he could pick me up. On the way home, I must have looked like a crazy person to anyone passing me. Look at this idiot girl grinning like the Cheshire cat while driving down the road. I floated into the house and up to my room. Then I quickly realized it had been far too long since I'd been on a date. Nervousness kicked in. My best friends were a phone call away, and twenty minutes later they were at my door.

"Help!" I pleaded when I opened it to let them in.

They squealed at me, and we acted like teenage school girls again as we headed up to my room to get me ready for my date.

By the time he pulled into my driveway, the girls had

managed to get me in a nice dress and strappy heels. We decided to pull my loose curls up and let some dangle here and there. A touch of make-up, and I was ready. Then, I hyperventilated because I was doing this; I was going on a real date. Now, as I said before, I had some not-serious dates or whatever, but I had no intentions of ever catching feelings again, so they were no big deal. With Ryan, though, I had the tingles. Something was there — some type of electricity between us. This is what had me panicking, I guess. The idea is that I might catch feelings again and therefore, get destroyed a second time. I could not let that happen. I don't think I could survive it again.

I picked up my phone to tell him I was going to have to cancel when Cassey jerked my phone away from me and held it high above her head. My vertically challenged self was not getting it back.

"No, Cass, you don't understand," I pleaded.

"Oh, I understand perfectly, Selena. You have spent years mourning your first love, and now you are finally at a strong enough place that you've even considered the possibility of maybe finding happiness with someone else. This is a breakthrough. We do not go backward, Sel; we move forward. You *are* going on this date."

"I can't. I really don't think I can do this, Cass."

She rolled her eyes. "You can, and you will! Besides, you can't back out now. He's getting ready to ring the doorbell."

Right on cue, the "*DING-DONG*" of the bell reverberated throughout the house. I closed my eyes in silent prayer.

"Maybe he'll just leave," I murmured to myself.

"SELENA," my mother sang up the stairs. "YOU HAVE A GUEST," she added in a quiet tone when she opened my bedroom door, "and he is a stunner! Nicely done, baby girl."

Her eyes sparkled mischievously. I groaned.

"Cold feet?" she asked, still grinning.

I nodded my head but allowed myself to be steered out of the room and down the stairs. I walked into the living room to find Ryan leaning over my father and both of them staring at the computer screen while Dad typed away. He was telling my father something that was making him very happy.

"Here she is," Mom piped up when I still hadn't announced my presence.

Ryan rose quickly; a perfect, shining smile drew up his face. He stared for a second, then reached back to the table and pulled up a bouquet, extending it out to me.

"You look beautiful," he said.

I brought the flowers to my face to smell them. "I have that in common with the flowers," I said, offering him a smile in return.

Mom took the flowers from me, claiming the need to put them in water as she made her way into the kitchen. There was an awkward silence before my dad's shout of victory exploded into the room. Dad jumped up from the chair, shook Ryan's hand vigorously, and clapped him on the back. He pointed at the screen and then looked at me, the happiness practically bursting from his face. He realized at once what I was in the room for and immediately reacted by stepping away from my date and taking a proper dad pose.

"So sorry, Selena bug. Uh, Ryan here was just helping with my draft."

I raised my eyebrows and looked from one to the other. I had no idea what they were talking about.

"Football," Dad blurted out, noticing my expression. "Fantasy Football, to be exact. I got the best QB available thanks to this guy." He gave Ryan another backslap.

"Oh," I said, "well, that's good then."

"Good? Selena, it's fantastic!" Dad exclaimed, raising his fists in triumph.

We laughed along with Dad. Mom came back in from the kitchen and scolded Dad for holding us up from our date. He mumbled out some agreement and apologized. Ryan moved around to the door and held it open for me. As I was walking out, I looked back and gave a wave to Amber and Cassey, who were both standing at the top of the stairs watching us go. He gave them a wave as well before closing the door.

"Best friends?" he asked, opening the car door.

"The best in the world," I told him, sliding into the seat.

We drove for about thirty-five minutes before I realized he was driving us into the city. Not long after that, we pulled into a wrap-in drive where a valet was waiting. The valet started to open my door, but Ryan waved him away as he reached down to do it himself. I took his hand and rose from the seat. He led me inside a beautiful restaurant and up to the maître d.

The man standing behind the podium was tall and skinny with a precisely trimmed gray mustache. His hair was steel gray and wrapped around his head from above one ear to above the other. There was no hair on top of his head. It was certainly the shiniest globe I'd ever seen. He drew himself up importantly and addressed us.

"Mr. James, I'm so glad you can join us this evening."

"Thank you, Maxwell. I'm glad to be here."

Maxwell smiled as he snapped his fingers and called out in Italian to one of the awaiting waiters behind him. A young man with black hair grabbed two menus before giving us a bow and indicating we should follow him.

"Enjoy your dinner," Maxwell called to us as we were led away.

Ryan gave him a smile and a nod, and then placed his

hand on the small of my back to lead me into the dining room.

We were seated by a window near the back. I liked the place because there was plenty of space in between the tables so that while the room was full, people weren't practically sitting on top of one another. Ryan held out my seat and made sure I was comfortable before settling in across from me.

"Everything here is delicious," he told me. "My aunt owns the restaurant, so I've tasted just about everything on the menu."

"Then what do you suggest?" I asked.

"I'm getting the fettuccini. It's so good."

He told me this with a starved look in his eye. I admitted to myself that he, so far, was a pretty good guy, and fettuccini, *yum*, my favorite. Finally, I relaxed and allowed myself to just have a nice date. After all, this didn't mean we were set for life, getting married or anything. It was just a date. There is no harm in that.

After a delicious dinner, which caused me to now have a nicely formed food baby, we drove back into Saint Caine and down to the boardwalk. The night was becoming more gorgeous. The sky was cloudless, so the stars were shining brightly, and the almost full moon was brilliant enough to light up the beach and surf. We walked and talked on the boardwalk itself, stopping to buy sweets and look around novelty shops. Before heading back to the car, we ended up barefoot, strolling this time on the beach itself, letting the cool surf lap at our feet. When we were near the pier, Ryan turned to me to look out at the ocean. He moved behind me and wrapped his arms around me, holding my hands in his own.

"I've had a wonderful night, Selena. Thank you for agreeing to come out with me."

"I've had a nice time, too. It's been such a long time; it's really nice."

He moved around to my side, and I shifted to face him. I noticed he looked concerned.

"Such a long time?" he asked me, furrowing his brows a bit.

I gently shook my head. "Never mind. It doesn't matter. I was just…" I sighed. "Thinking out loud."

He nodded his head up and down a couple of times. His hands rubbed up and down my arms. "Chilled?" he asked.

"Not really, maybe a little."

I knew it. He had felt the bumps on my arms, and instead of realizing they were because of my reaction to his touch, his scent and goodness, the very feel of his rock-hard chest at my shoulder blades, he thought it was because I was cold. I had to cover that up.

"We should go then," he said, "but first, I want to go ahead and ask you just two quick questions."

"Alright."

"Alright," he said as well, "first question. Since you admitted to having a nice time tonight, will you consider having a second date with me?"

I laughed a little and nodded my head. "Yes, I will have a second date with you."

He let out an exaggerated sigh of relief. "Yes," he added to it, letting the *s* linger out a little.

"And…" I said laughing, "the second question is?"

I watched his face as the smile and laughter faded out and his eyes clouded over with intensity. He licked his lips, and I stared as the tip of his tongue slid slowly back into his mouth.

"I've been dying to kiss you since I met you," he admitted. "May I kiss you now?"

His question was so soft and so serious. Everything about this night with him was playful and light-hearted. He made me comfortable and spoke as if we'd known each other for years, even though we were asking questions and answering with words that would give us insight into one another and who we were. Under this bright moon, with grainy, wet sand squishing against our feet and the chilly ocean water sliding the sand away with each receding wave, he was serious. I could see the strong desire in his eyes and noticed the twitch of his jawline as he was doing all he could to patiently await and respect my response. His thumb slid over my bicep, and there went my do-dah. Oh Lord, here we go again.

"Yes." I breathed and barely spoke the word out of my mouth when his hands were cupping my face and his lips were on mine.

The kiss was gentle but passionate at the same time. Heat radiated up my body from my toes to neck. Sliding an arm around my waist, he pulled me closer to him, now using the other hand to cup the back of my neck while deepening our kiss. I was certain one of us was going to pass out from lack of oxygen when he reluctantly slid his lips from my own while placing his forehead against mine. We were both panting.

"Holy," he breathed.

"Mm-hmm," I agreed.

It was close to one in the morning when he dropped me back at home. At the door, he took two more passionate kisses before sliding his hand from mine. With a sly smile, I opened the door and quietly shut it before locking it again. When I entered my room, I wasn't surprised to see a lipstick-written note on my vanity mirror from Cassey and Amber.

All the details
Tomorrow!

I laughed out loud and threw myself back onto my bed. That night, I slept peacefully. I slid right into sleep without a care in the world. Would I ever learn?

sixteen

ARE YOU KIDDING ME?

W ell, I did it. I let down a little bit of the wall I kept around my heart. Just a little bit, though. Don't worry, I'm not stupid. Misguided, naïve, and often non-confrontational, but not stupid. At least, I'd like to think so anyway.

I've now had several dates with Ryan, and I am thrilled to say they have all been wonderful. He hasn't strayed from being the good guy I've met. My job has been amazing as well. I've written several pieces for the Syndicate, but if you'd picked it up, you wouldn't know it. I prefer to use a pen name. This keeps me from having to answer questions from the public when I am out and about. If we lived in the city, it would be one thing, but Saint Caine is no city.

Around six months after the start of my job my boss, Mr. Darnell, decided it was time to see what I was made of. He informed me that the little fluff pieces I'd been writing were good, but he could see the potential for some serious, informative writing there. So, as of that moment, I was to interview the man behind the means. In other words, money was coming in for a brand-new Saint Caine High

School football field and stadium renovations. Some old bigwigs from down south had roots in our school and wanted to give back. They are opening a large plant out in the Industrial Park and are using their good fortune to contribute to our community and gain support. Truth be told, this corporation is a steel plant, and that meant lots of jobs for Saint Caine and the surrounding area.

"You are to be at this address at one o'clock sharp."

I leaned forward and took the paper from Mr. Darnell. "Who am I interviewing?"

"I don't know yet," answered Darnell gruffly, slinging up his pants by the belt. I thought he would soon need a bigger belt, but thoughts like that you keep to yourself. Especially if you want to remain employed. I cleared my throat and frowned at him.

"I have to know who I am interviewing, or should I just go in and ask every random person a question and type my article off of their responses?"

"Nice biting wit, Ayers," he ground out. His voice sounded like that of an old record player. Gravelly and scratching. He coughed and sniffed while leaning on his desk and folding his hands together. "Save the smart retorts for the article. When you go in, just tell reception that you are the reporter from the Syndicate to give an interview about the football field donation. When I was last on the phone with them, they couldn't decide whether we would be interviewing the man in charge or one of his lackeys. So, as I said before, I don't know yet. I'll find out when you do. Now get to it, gypsy. You've got over half an hour's drive, and its already noon."

"Guess I'll grab a bite on the way then," I huffed, standing up and snatching my things from the chair.

"No. Don't do that. Chew gum now and eat after. I don't want dragon breath ruining a good interview."

I turned back to him at the door. "Nice biting wit, Darnell," I quipped, slinging the door open.

Mr. Darnell just snorted and waved me away. That was as good a dismissal as any.

———

The building I pulled up to wasn't anything fancy at all. This was probably because it was a rented facility while the plant and offices were being built further down the road. I stepped into the square brick monstrosity and pushed the elevator to the fourth floor. When the doors opened, I walked out onto a carpeted hall floor with a reception desk directly in front of the elevator. A fit brunette with a strong jaw smiled at me as I approached the desk. I smiled back.

"Hello. Welcome to Generations Steel; how may I help you?" she asked. She was very pleasant.

"I'm from the Syndicate," I told her, "I'm supposed to be interviewing with one of your department heads, I believe."

"Oh, yes. We've been expecting you," she started, then frowned as she clicked on her keyboard. "I'm sorry," she apologized. "I don't have you here; I have a Mr. Sel Mayer."

I laughed a little. "That is me. I use a pen name when I write. It's just Sel Mayer, not a mister."

"Oh, okay. So that *is* you." She was relieved. "I thought I was losing it there for a second." She clicked the keyboard again and then came around the desk to lead me down the hall. "I'm not sure which one of our heads you'll be interviewing," she told me as we walked. "They still haven't let me know, which makes it seem as though we aren't very organized, but I assure you we are on top of things. They just can't decide who would make the best representation for our business." She stopped at a door with a plaque that read V.P. and opened it. I thanked her as I walked past and headed into the room.

"Can I get you anything? Water or a soda? It could be a few minutes before anyone arrives."

I looked back at her, taking a seat across from the desk and rummaging through my bag for my pen and pad. "No, thank you," I told her, chewing the last dregs of my gum before tossing it in the trash. "*My boss is a dink*", I thought to myself.

She gave me another smile and closed the door. I looked around the office, making notes as I did. The desk was made of beautiful mahogany wood. There was another name plate on it, once again only displaying V.P., a pen holder, and a wooden box containing what looked like important papers. A sleek black computer monitor and keyboard. One large desk calendar, from which I sneakily read a few appointments and notes. It turns out the V.P. will be attending our Christmas festivities at the Syndicate this year. I made a note. I was just sweeping the pictures on the walls when I heard a deep voice and the voice of the receptionist in the hall.

"...no more than a half hour at most, Dawna, oh, and," his voice lowered a bit, "what's this guy like? Snobbish or overly friendly?"

The receptionist laughed heartily. "Oh, I think you'll be pleasantly surprised," she said.

I heard the door handle turn, so I placed my things on the chair beside me and turned to stand up and greet him. I plastered my one-hundred-watt smile on my face and held out my hand. He came through the door, dusting something off his shirt, just before raising his head to greet me. My smile dropped, my eyes widened, and then everything went black.

You know what I hate to be woken from? Not necessarily the dream stage of sleep, but those moments before and after. There is nothing to bother you or take your attention; there are no hidden demons lurking to rear their ugly heads in the form of some monster that is a representation of some underlying fear. That's a peaceful place. You are relaxed, and all is well. I hate to be woken from that blissful stage, especially at this moment in time, where the demons and underlying fears are waiting to face me in reality. I scrunch my face in protest, deliberately doing all I could not to open my eyes.

"She's coming around," I heard a nice voice say. I knew that voice, too. It was the receptionist.

"Thank goodness, it's about time. Will you bring some water, please?"

"Yes, sir," she answered. I heard footsteps and then the closing of a door.

There was rustling to my right. I was lying down, probably on the expensive leather couch I had seen in the office.

"If you are waiting for me to leave, you are going to be there for a while," the male voice informed me. "This is my office, and I've spent the last two nights here."

I steeled my nerves, swallowed, and then opened my eyes. Texas Conrad the Fourth was standing over me, holding a cold pack in his right hand. I glared up at him. His lips went up in a smirk as he placed the pack on my head. We stared at each other for too long before he shoved his hands in his pockets and spoke.

"I have every intention of telling you how wonderful it is to see you, Selena, but I'd rather you not faint. I can call a doctor."

"No need. I'm fine," I shot, attempting to raise myself upward.

His hands found my shoulders and eased me back down. My head swam a bit, so I didn't object too much.

"You're not fine. A person doesn't faint without reason," he snapped.

"Oh, there's a reason," I growled. "It has a lot to do with unexpected people appearing before my eyes."

"You were just as unexpected for me; although I must say I'm thrilled, I'm still not the one lying on the couch because of it."

"Well, that's most likely because…" I stammered as irritation flowed through my voice. "Because you've probably eaten today!" I finished the sentence, flinging my hands out to emphasize the point.

"You haven't eaten anything?" he complained, leaning towards me as he did so. "Honestly, reporters never learn. You lot will forsake everything just to get a story. I'll have Dawna grab you something off the cart."

"No, Lord, no, please." I flung myself upward in protest. "I'll get myself something on the way back."

The dizziness was gone, and I was able to get up from the couch and make my way over to the desk and chair where my things still sat.

"You're leaving?" Tex asked, watching me with interest.

"That's the plan," I said, raising an eyebrow as I stuffed my pen and pad back into my satchel.

Tex moved behind his desk. "Won't your boss be upset if you come back empty-handed?"

"My boss," I started to argue, but then I thought about Darnell and how he was determined that I write this piece to prove myself for future and bigger column space. Defeated, I took a huge breath, weighed my options, and finally settled on just doing the interview as quickly as possible and getting out of there.

"Fine!" I snapped. "We'll do the interview."

Tex's eyes lit up, and a dazzling smile spread across his face. Dawna came in the door and brought a pitcher of ice water along with a tall glass. She poured it full as I got my things back out and settled myself in the chair. I thanked her before she left, then picked up the glass and drained it. Tex watched my every movement. I was determined not to make eye contact.

"So," I said, "Mr. Conrad…"

"Selena?" he asked, tilting his head to the side. This time, I stared him straight in the eyes. Just this once, to let him know I was controlling this.

"Mr. Conrad…" I said again.

He held up his hands in surrender, spun a little to the right in his chair, and nodded for me to continue.

"The best way to tell a story is to start at the beginning. As I am telling your story to the people of Saint Caine, I desire to let them know what has brought such a benevolent benefactor to our little town and why the display of such staggering generosity. We'll get the background. Tell me about yourself and how you came to be who you are today."

"I would think you could answer that yourself," he said softly to me.

I closed my eyes and breathed, with my pen poised at my pad.

"Very well," he said, righting his chair and leaning forward. "I am Texas Conrad the Fourth. My father and the generations before him are also Texas Conrads. My great-grandfather struck oil while digging for a well on his plantation. He used his great fortune to start a business empire. We started with little gas stations here and there and, over time, grew into a great corporation. Texacon stations are erected all over the United States. Each male heir in the family is part of the business and takes their rightful place in keeping things running smoothly."

"No matter the cost," I murmured.

"What was that?" he asked.

"Oh, nothing," I replied sweetly, keeping my eyes closed in his direction but faking a smile.

"Did you say…" he started, but I interrupted him.

"Mr. Conrad, you mentioned your great fortune in the gas industry, but this current venture is a steel mill. How did that come about, exactly?"

There was silence. I was very much aware that he was staring at me, practically willing me to look at him. I refused. My ears were burning and no doubt bright red. I was sweating and making sure I took deliberate breaths to keep myself calm.

He finally cleared his throat to answer. "Yes, well, we have gone as far as we hoped with the oil and gas industry. It is a thriving business, and we're pleased, but it is our goal to be valuable to communities, even to the very nation. There are many places where we can achieve that, not just in oil and gas." He leaned forward a bit, being sure to hold my attention as he spoke. "You see, the idea first came to me years ago when we were forced to watch those videos in school about the attacks on the U.S. during 9/11. I had thought about it then but never pursued it any further. Until just a couple of years ago, when I saw yet another one of those videos on television. Again, I pondered, what if we could create steel that could with-stand the hardest blasts and the most intense heat," he emphasized, holding up a finger, "and what if we could do it here, in the U.S., using our materials and our people? We want the United States to profit above all else in our industry. Every business deal, every merger is on our soil with our citizens."

I narrowed my eyes and gave him a vicious look. "Mergers are very important in big business, aren't they?" I asked.

Tex's brows furrowed, and he licked his lips. When they parted again, I didn't give him time to come up with an answer. Next question.

"You are donating quite a lot of money to Saint Caine and its school system, in particular, the football program. Why us? Why that program?"

He didn't smile anymore, nor did he prostrate himself in different ways to seem more important. Instead, he just watched me as he answered.

"Saint Caine is my alma mater. I graduated as the quarterback of our football team. We were the championship team, but it was no secret that the gear and field were extremely outdated. I always told my teammates that if I ever got to where I could make a difference for the future soldiers of Saint Caine, I would start with the football program."

"I see. Is it fair to say…" I began, but this time it was I who was interrupted.

"You see, Ms. Ayers," he said, capturing my eyes for the first time. I couldn't look away. I wanted to, Lord knows I wanted to, but I just couldn't. "Saint Caine," he told me, "means so much more to me than just a school where I once played ball. I have roots here, memories that are more precious to me than just 'the good ole' days. Saint Caine is the very embodiment of my happiness. She's where I began to truly live. Unfortunately, I made my mistakes with her, so I pushed myself to make this happen because if I couldn't make right what I had done with her, then I could at least do right *by* her. Make sure her memory never fades."

My mouth parted open with unsaid words. In the quiet moment, just a slight pull of a smile tugged up the right corner of Tex's mouth. My heart was hollow. As a writer, I knew a metaphor when I heard one, and all sorts of feelings were jockeying for a place in my body as I processed what he had just implied.

The sound of the door opening broke the spell. Another gruff voice was calling back to Dawna, telling her he'd *"like some coffee, please"*. Tex looked up at the man entering his office.

"Are you busy, Tex?" he asked. "I can come back if needed."

"I'm in the middle of…"

"That's alright," I quickly piped up. I rose as fast as possible, grabbing my bag and fishing out my keys as I spoke. "I'm sure I've got plenty to work with." I moved to the door, pulling it back as I left. "Thank you for your time, Mr. Conrad."

I left the both of them there, staring after me as I shut the door and shuffled back down the hall.

"I'm sorry, Tex. I didn't mean to frighten the lady off," the newcomer told him.

"You didn't, Mr. Ewing. She had mentioned needing to leave not too much earlier than when you arrived. What can I do for you?" Tex asked him, moving around the desk to pick up a pencil that had fallen when I had bumped the desk accidentally, hurrying to leave.

He bent down and paused, noticing not only the pencil but my writing pad that had fallen as well. He smiled to himself, picked them both up, and straightened. While he and Mr. Ewing talked, Tex placed the pad on his desk before leaning against it. Mr. Ewing went into a big spiel about the groundbreaking. Tex was attentive and listened, but as he did so, he let his mind wander back to my face. I hadn't changed a bit to him. Sure, I was older, but still so very beautiful. He had so much he wanted to say, but I had been so difficult and forceful, and honestly, he was afraid the wrong word or approach would send me bolting for the door. I had practically done that, hadn't I? He reached over and pulled the pad back up from the desk before sliding it in his shirt pocket. He would see me again. Now that he knew I was back home, he would make sure of it.

Out on the road, I was lead-footing it. I didn't want a speeding ticket, but I also wanted to get as far away as I could as quickly as I could. My throat was tightening, and my eyes were burning. What had just happened? *Did* that just happen? Had I actually sat across from Texas Conrad, the very man who caused me to skip town, finish my education online, and take years to make myself come back to town, *AND*, on top of that, did I just interview him?

I was hyperventilating again. Knowing I would need time to pull myself together, I turned the car into the first parking lot I saw. It turned out to be an outlet mall, so there was plenty of parking far away from onlookers. I put the car in park, leaned my head against the steering wheel, and took long, slow, deep breaths. *"Just calm down,"* I thought to myself, *"Breath girl. You are going to be fine."* After a few minutes, my heart stopped hammering against my chest. Fresh tears rolled down my face, and I began sobbing. It was a strange and, I suspect, eerie sight to anyone who might have seen me. I was sitting alone in a car, sobbing uncontrollably and laughing at the same time. I was losing it.

If it hadn't been for my phone ringing, I might have let myself spill the rest of the way over into complete hysterics, but as it was, the phone rang and Ryan's handsome face filled my screen. I had no choice but to get it together this time. It reached the third ring before I gathered my wits about me and answered in my fakest *"everything is perfect"* voice.

"Hey, you," I said, forcing more enthusiasm than necessary.

"Well, hi, beautiful. It seems someone is having a good day."

"Not too bad. Darnell sent me on my first big assignment, so there's that."

"Wow," he said happily, "that's great. We both know you deserve it."

"Sure," I said, "we can celebrate tonight if you want."

"Awe, babe, that's one of the reasons why I was calling. I'm going to have to ask for a rain check."

"Ok. Is everything alright?"

"Yes. Everything is fine; it's just that we acquired some new clients today, and Harmon wants us to all have dinner and discuss the finer points of our representation. He just wants to schmooze his new piggy bank."

I laughed. "I understand. We'll do it another night. You said that was just one of the reasons, though; what was the other reason?"

"I just wanted to hear your beautiful voice."

I smiled genuinely this time, and after hearing his voice, I was feeling a lot better. "It's good to hear your voice too," I told him.

We talked a little longer, but eventually I told him I had to go and start getting busy on this piece.

"Alright, I'll call you tonight if it's not too late."

"Bye," I told him, pushing the phone to hang up the call.

That was just what I needed to get my head back on track. So, I saw Texas Conrad today. Big deal. I mean, it's a small town, and honestly, I figured at some point I might see him roaming around somewhere. Cassey and Amber had already informed me that his parents still live in the same big house I had visited all those years ago. I knew it would probably happen eventually. I just wasn't prepared for it to be today. Still, it happened, and I survived.

I gave my head a mental nod. It's time for me to get focused, write the piece to the best of my ability, and move forward. The worst was now behind me. I pulled my satchel apart and reached in for my pad to peruse my notes. My bag was a lot like the ones mentioned in those wizard books. I could stick my hand in it and pull out anything from a piece of gum to a full-size hair dryer. After coming up empty one too many times, I went all out and upended the bag to let the contents spill onto the seat. Before I finished rummaging through the mess, I admitted what I knew to be true all along. I had left my notepad back in Tex's office. This day sucked. I hated it and was ready for it to be over already. I turned the car on, pushed the gas, and headed off the interstate to the back road I knew would bring me around to my house.

Truthfully, it was my parents' other house. They bought it about a couple of months ago when the previous owners decided Florida was calling their name. Since the house was directly behind my parents and a cute little two-bedroom perfect for an early twenties girl just starting in life, they bought it, and I pay all the bills. It works for me. At one point, I accused them of being afraid I might run away again, but they just told me they had no idea what I was talking about as they shrugged their shoulders and went back to playing cards. I love them, but they are horrible liars and need to learn to not grin at each other when they are trying to get one over on me.

"Whatever! I'll live in the house," I agreed, "but I'm still eating here whenever I want."

"Deal," they both said.

I pulled into my driveway and called Darnell's office to let him know I was home and wouldn't be back in until the morning. I love my little chocolate brown home with its small front porch and creamy mocha shutters. There's a big glass window to the left of the porch, and I love to pull the curtains back and let the morning sun shine in while I enjoy my hot tea and go over my notes before work. I was admiring my flower bed and garden gnomes while waiting for Darnell to reply.

"Excellent Ayers. Good idea. Get where you can concentrate and hammer out that article. I want the first notes on my desk by nine," he demanded.

"But I…"

Of course, I didn't get to finish. Mr. Darnell was no-nonsense, get to the point, make it happen, captain!

I rolled my eyes heavenward before dragging myself up the two steps onto my porch. As I walked through the door, I let everything lay where it fell. Shoes off in the entryway, bag dropped by the end of the chair, jacket slung over the chair, and shirt pulled out of the skirt before I landed on the couch.

"Today sucked," I said to no one.

seventeen

NEVER LOOK A GIFT HORSE IN THE MOUTH!

After using the address so conveniently left behind on my belongings, Tex was able to easily figure out that I was living in the small house behind my parents. As soon as he concluded his brief meeting with Mr. Ewing, he went right to work on making sure he got to see me again.

He drove all the way to his parent's house first to talk to his mother. He knew he was going to have to handle everything that happened next very carefully. He drove around the driveway and stopped outside of the estate. When he walked inside, he found his mother in the sitting room, drinking sweet tea and reading one of her novels. He often teased her about her choice of reading material, even going so far as to call it smut, which always earned him a smack and an admonishment from her.

She was curled at the end of the white plush sofa, wearing one of her comfy jogger suits. This one was burgundy. Her soft eyes crinkled at the corners with a smile when she looked up and saw him coming into the room.

"Well," she cooed, "what a nice surprise this is. I didn't expect to see you until the weekend."

Tex strolled over to her, bent to kiss her cheek, and moved to the chair across from her. She leaned up and placed her tea on the coaster resting on the gleaming glass coffee table. He wasted no time in filling her in.

"I had to come and see you," he said, beaming a brilliantly happy smile. "I have the most wonderful news."

Her eyebrows rose with interest. "Really? Then please tell me; I can hardly stand the suspense." She moved to an upright position, ready to hear what had her son so excited. Tex unbuttoned his suit jacket and leaned back, sliding his hands along the plush fabric of the chair and smiling broadly.

"Guess, just guess who interviewed me today for the Syndicate."

Her eyebrow arched. "Texas, you know good, and well, I haven't the foggiest about those reporters. Just tell me already."

"It was Selena Marie Ayers," he drew out, raising his own eyebrow in a perfect match to her own.

His words had the effect he thought they would. His mother's hands came up to her face as her eyes widened in surprise. "Oh, my. Oh, Texas, were you really? She's back home; she's actually here in Saint Caine?"

He nodded his head up and down, a bit of laughter bubbling out of his throat. "Yes, yes, she is, and she's so beautiful mother, even more so now. She's still smart and funny, and…" he stopped talking, swallowing hard as he rubbed his hands together. His mother leaned forward, her own hands worrying each other.

"What?" she asked, concern lacing her words. "Texas, what is it?"

"Well, to be perfectly honest, I was going to add that I'm pretty sure she still hates me."

"I don't believe that for one bit," she drawled, waving

off his comment as if it were an annoying fly at her head, "not one bit at all."

Texas looked straight at her, gave her a dramatic eye roll, and said, "You weren't there today. You didn't see the way she looked at me or hear the digs she took at me during that interview."

"Why don't you start at the beginning? Tell me everything that happened from the moment you saw her again."

So he did. He started his story with the moment he opened the door and looked at the big brown eyes he'd been dreaming about for almost a decade of his life now. He had stopped in his tracks just as I had blinked twice before collapsing onto the floor before him. He had rushed to scoop me up and carry me over to the couch, snatching one of the magazines from the low mahogany coffee table in front of it and waving it over my face as if that would miraculously wake me up. When I hadn't woken in sufficient time, he'd gone to the door and yelled for Dawna, who came running so fast it surprised him. Looking back, he assumed it had probably been the urgency in his tone.

His mother leaned back into the couch as he continued his story, further telling her that after he had quickly explained to Dawna what had happened to me, his receptionist informed him that the same thing had happened to a girlfriend of hers when she found out the guy she'd been dating for over a year had a kid. It was the sudden shock that caused her friend to forget to breathe and, therefore, resulted in her passing out. Once Tex had heard that, he deduced that since he was shocked at seeing me, it stood to reason that I was even more shocked at seeing him. So, he took Dawna's advice and wet a rag to gently pat against my head until I finally came out of it. He only had to wait about twenty minutes.

"And then she agreed to the interview, which was where

I realized she was still severely ticked at me," he added, holding up a finger to stop his mother's words from coming out of her opening lips. Leaning forward, he gave her a sly smile as he pulled the notepad from his inside pocket. He let it drop onto the table and tapped it as he continued, "but she left this behind. I know where she is this time, and I am not going to let her get away from me again."

His mother took a deep breath as she eyed the pad he had tapped. "Well," she said, "that is quite a tale, but son, I really think you should think this through. I know every part of you wants to just rush right over there and say all the things you didn't get to before."

Tex opened his mouth to say something, but she waved her hand in the air, indicating for him to let her finish. He closed his mouth and waited as she did.

"What I'm trying to say is that she has had seven years to rehash that day over and over again. Being a woman and having somewhat of an idea as to what she has gone through, I can assure you that having you show up and wanting the opportunity to explain yourself is not going to go over well."

He rose up from the chair, shoved his hand through that perfect white-gold hair, and began to pace. "Then what do you suggest? I can't just do nothing."

"I understand that, and I'm not telling you to do nothing; I'm simply suggesting you find a different approach."

"Okay," he said, stopping to look down at her on the couch. The helplessness on his face was enough to break any mother's heart. "What do you suggest I do? What should I say?"

That's what led to him going to our once favorite Italian restaurant and picking up dinner. His mother's suggestion was that instead of showing up and all but insisting she hear him out, he should instead work on gaining the friendship back that he lost. Hopefully, by showing up with the food, she wouldn't send him away, and he could get the time he needed to talk with her. He'd use finishing the interview as an excuse, and once they'd managed to be civil to one another, he'd work the conversation around to apologizing because he owed her that.

At the restaurant, he saw her mother and father laughing and talking at a table in the back of the restaurant. He made sure he kept himself firmly behind the large plant by the hostess podium while he waited for his order. Seeing them was another stroke of luck for him. If they were out, then that meant that Selena was on her own for dinner. With a triumphant smile, he paid for his food and, anonymously, her parent's meal before sauntering back to his car.

Not a half-hour later, he was pulling onto her street. The sound of gravel crunching under tires filled the space until he drove onto the smooth pavement of her driveway. He shut the car off and looked around. It was a modest home with a porch and lovely, clean windows. A small bed of flowers was planted off the side of the steps in beautiful spring colors, with a couple of gnomes watching over it. He eyed the door, considering whether or not she would hold it open for him or slam it in his face. Blowing out a breath, he grabbed the food bags, exited the car, and headed up the steps. It was now or never. A slightly trembling finger pushed the inviting white button beside the door.

eighteen

SERIOUSLY?

I had crashed where my body met the couch. The sound of the doorbell woke me up, followed by the knocking. I sat up and yawned while reaching for the coffee table. I had planned on checking my phone, but it wasn't there. Then I remembered my slugfest on the couch and my willingness not to care what ended up where. The doorbell rang again.

"Coming," I called out. I figured it was one of the girls. I had told them I was supposed to go out with Ryan tonight, but if they've been texting or calling and I haven't been answering, they were bound to come find me. "I'm alright, guys," I started saying as I unlocked the door. "I just fell asleep."

"At least you're rested but tell me this, did you ever eat?"

I am wide awake now. Tex was on my porch, holding a takeout bag from the one place he knew I couldn't resist. He was still wearing the suit from earlier, but the jacket was open and his tie was loosened at his neck. He looked just as good disheveled as he did dapper. I stood in place, staring at him.

"You could invite me in," he said.

"What! How even?" I mumbled, dragging my falling hair back out of my face.

"Normally, the person in the home says to the person standing outside, '*Come in*'."

I narrowed my eyes and frowned at him. "You know what I mean."

"Ah, that. You left this when you sped out of my office earlier." He pulled my notepad from his pocket and held it out to me. "Your information is in the very front. You might want to be more careful with that."

I snatched the pad from him and tossed it on the entryway table underneath the large rectangle mirror. "Thank you," I said.

"You're very welcome." He told me and then held up the bag. "Is Fettuccini still your favorite?"

He knew it was my favorite. Oh, he knew. This man knew everything about me, and I could tell he was going to use that information to his advantage. "Look, Tex," I started, holding out my hand as if it would keep him on the porch. "I interviewed you, and thank you for allowing me your time to do that, but the interview is over now. I'll write the article, and I promise you that I won't put anything disparaging or cruel in it. I'm a professional; there's no need to make sure I behave."

"I'm only here to make sure you eat."

"There is food in my kitchen."

"I seriously doubt that," he snorted with a laugh. "Your mother is less than sixty feet from you. I'd say you eat there about every night, but lucky for me, I happen to know they are out."

I tightened my lips into a painfully thin line. *Dang it*, he was right. I was supposed to be going out tonight, so Mom and Dad decided to have a date of their own.

Tex raised his eyebrows and moved forward. "It's just food, Selena, and we can finish the interview. I saw you had a few questions left."

"You'll leave after?" I asked, but in a way *told* him what was going to happen.

"Unless you ask me to stay," he said.

"I won't."

"I figured that."

He moved past me and into the house. The living area opened up right off the entryway, so you just went around the wall to step down into it. The kitchen was past the living room and to the right. I followed Tex to it but lingered in the opening between the kitchen and hall. He put the bag on my counter and began pulling food out of it.

"In which cabinet do you keep the plates?" he asked me, turning to look at me as he opened the first of the two meals.

Giving in, I rolled my eyes and walked over to the cabinet above the microwave. I pulled out two plates from there, and then I opened the drawer by the refrigerator to get silverware. Tex was making himself at home. He opened the fridge, got two sodas, and brought them over to the counter. I brought one of the stools around to one side for him before walking back around to sit on the other. I was hoping this was letting him know I had no desire for him to be any closer to me than that, but he just took his seat and began putting food on the plates. Men are hopeless. He can't even tell that I was trying to be a jerk.

We dug into the food quietly at first. I'll admit I was starving, and it was so good. Like, so very good. I can't even...

"Thank you," I finally told him, after stuffing my face.

"My pleasure."

I looked up to see him watching me, so I wiped my

mouth, grabbed a pen and paper from beside my virtual assistant device—yes, I had one of those—and started on the questions I hadn't asked yet.

"Let's see. I asked you about your beginnings and your current endeavors. That leaves how the mill came about after conception and your personal life. We'll start with the conception. Once you had the initial idea, how did Generations get created?"

Tex finished chewing and swallowing. He was continuing to eat, but talking to me all the same. I mean, he wasn't gross about it, like chewing with half-masticated noodles leaking out of his mouth or anything, but he was eating and talking just as we always had back then. When we just hung out together.

"That's where the first designs and development came in," he said. "Mr. Ewing had a couple of connections from his businesses out in California, so he made some calls, and not too long after that, we had investors."

Tex took a drink of soda when he finished talking. This was my opportunity to ask another question. I finished scribbling some notes and flipped the page for fresh space.

"Mr. Ewing," I said, writing his name at the top, "so he's continued to be an avid partner all these years?"

"Yes. He's the one who came up with the name Generations. See, he knew that dad and I are the third and fourth in our family line, and it turns out he's the second in his so he thought, what better name for the company than to acknowledge the generations who brought it to life?" He took another drink and swallowed. "He's a good man, Jack Ewing."

"A good man, yeah," I spat before I could help myself, "especially when it comes to treating people fairly and equally and all that." I took a drink as I looked at Tex for his response.

Tex's face took on that knowing expression, and his words were softer as he spoke. "He is nothing like my father; I can assure you of that, and he loves his son-in-law and grandson."

I pulled at my notes and frowned. "Who are they?" I asked him, not finding mention of them anywhere in the things I had jotted down.

"They're not in your notes," he answered, twirling his fork to twist up some noodles. "This is the first time we've discussed them. They are Elizabeth's husband and child, and they are both people of color."

I looked at the clock for an excuse to look anywhere but at him. I certainly wasn't expecting to hear that Elizabeth Ewing, the famous model and daughter of Mr. Wealthy Texas business tycoon, not only married a man of color but also had a child. I mean, when it came to Tex's father, heaven forbid. I am only of gypsy ancestry, and we know how that went. This news did several different things to me, none of which I wanted to acknowledge at the moment. Music sounded from the other room. Tex got up to move out there, but I got past him and assured him everything was fine. "It's my phone; that's Cassey's ringtone."

It was one of those bumpin' R&B hits centered around a girl's awesome backside. Don't judge me. She demanded I use it. I answered the call and listened as Cass told me if I hadn't picked up when I did, she was coming over there to find me. I promised her I was fine and had fallen asleep. When she asked about Ryan, I told her how he had to cancel for the night. She then asked if I had eaten since she saw my mom and dad out and about. I laughed at her, casting my eyes on the ceiling, as I realized everyone knew me too well. We hung up, and I went back to the kitchen. Tex wasn't in there, so I checked the bathroom before making my way to the living room.

He was on my couch, changing the channels on my television.

"Um, are we going to finish the interview?" I asked him, thumbing back behind myself and indicating the kitchen we had been in.

"Can we finish in here? I want to see if our ad has made the channels yet."

"It has," I told him, coming into the room and sitting in the chair opposite the couch. "I saw it the day before yesterday. I didn't know *you* were a part of Generations Steel at the time, but I saw the ad just the same."

"Ah well, that's good then. I hadn't seen it yet."

He flicked a few more channels, and I became agitated as he did this. I looked at him. He was still so perfectly handsome. His jawline was still as strong as it had been, even though his shape had gone from slightly boyish to a definite man's build. The controller was in his right hand, and I followed up his arm to see the indentation of muscle under the tight-fit dress shirt. That was enough. I closed my eyes and put my head in my hand. My arm rested against the chair's arm.

"I think I have plenty of material to write a strong article in your favor, Tex," I said. "We can call it a night."

"I searched for you, Selena. I tried everything I could," he scoffed. "I even begged my father to use his resources to help me find you."

"What?" I asked, placing my hands in my lap and making myself look at him. I shouldn't have done that. He leaned back onto the couch, his hands clasped in front of him, and his eyes were glassy. The way eyes get when you have tears but refuse to let them fall. "What are you talking about, Tex?" I asked again, shaking my head.

"You know what I am talking about. After you left, after that night, I came straight to your house. I searched for you. I drove all night and into the next day. I wanted to find you so badly, to explain…to talk to you."

"Don't Tex. Just…don't." My shoulders slumped, and I sighed heavily. I didn't want to do this then, and I don't want to do this now. "It's done; it's over with. Seven years have passed." I told him with finality.

"It shouldn't have been seven minutes," he spat, leaning forward in the chair.

"It shouldn't have happened at all," I shot back, tossing my hand out in a cut-across motion. I felt heat rising up my neck and knew I was getting into something I didn't want to.

Tex got up from the couch and began pacing in front of it. He rubbed his neck before turning to me in agitation.

"I know that!" he confessed. "I know it should never have happened, but it did, and I wanted to make it right; I wanted to fix it. I tried."

"There's no fixing it," I informed him, building anger with my words. "You broke my heart, Tex; you utterly destroyed me, and you honestly think you could have found me somewhere; said some rehearsed words, and it would have made everything alright?"

"Nothing I said would have made a difference to the hurt I caused you. I get that. I *know* that," he argued, stopping to face me. "I'm not trying to justify myself or my actions in any way, Selena. I just want… just need…" he huffed a breath and looked up to the ceiling. After a few moments, he sat down hard on the edge of the couch. I was at the edge of the chair. My eyes were burning with anger and years of hidden hurt.

"I need you to forgive me," he said softly, his voice breaking as he did, and suddenly he wasn't irritated or confused. He was broken, and in that instant I saw the brokenness in him that everyone else must have seen in me all those years ago.

I swallowed and looked away, pursing my lips. *"How dare he?"* I thought. *"How dare he come into my home after all these years and ask me to forgive him for what he did to me. To even think of showing me any pain that might induce sympathy from me. I gave him parts of me that I can never get back, and he treated those gifts as if they were gum under his shoe."* I could feel the anger scorching my face as I looked back at him. He was staring at me still, pleading at me with his eyes. I could rage at him. I could jump over the coffee table and hit him, beat him with my fists until his body hurt the way mine did that awful night all those years ago. But then what? What would happen after I unleashed the fury I wanted to? After I said every mean and evil thing I'd been holding in? The fact is that no matter what I said or did, nothing would go back and keep me from the past years I'd lived. It was useless; there was no point. I acquiesced.

"Fine," I said, standing up and holding out my arms. "You need forgiveness, then you can have it. I forgive you."

He stood up as well. His jaw twitched, and he narrowed his eyes a little. He always did that when he suspected I was up to something. "You do? Really?"

I shook my head back and forth and held up my hands before dropping them again, my lips that thin line once again. An exasperated sigh finally forced its way out of my mouth.

"Yes, I guess… or no, but what does it matter? I mean, what's done is done."

"Selena," he started, moving around the table to come into my space.

I jerked over and held out my hand to stop him from advancing. Hot tears were threatening to spill over my lids.

"No," I told him, "don't, okay? Just listen," I begged,

moving further away, as if at any moment he would catch me up, and Lord help me if he did such a thing. "I know you think you need my forgiveness, but you don't. You're doing great. You've got your own business now; you're successful, and you've probably got a ton of women just throwing themselves at you." I made myself take a deep breath — just a pause to collect myself and calm my tone. After closing and opening my eyes, I looked right at him. "So, I'm irrelevant. I mean, my forgiveness, or not having it, hasn't kept you from getting to where you are today, so it shouldn't matter. It's done. I'll just go my way, and you can just keep going yours."

"I couldn't find you," he insisted. "I tried Selena; for weeks I tried."

"And if you had?" I argued back, calmness already gone as quickly as it came. "What then? We would be in no different place than we are right now."

"I can't believe that. I won't."

"But it's true, right? You say you need something, but I can't give it to you. I never could, and I don't think I ever will. I've had to live day in and day out with those last few months and that horrible last day. I'll live with it for the rest of my life. You just have to live with being the one who did it. The one who decided that instead of fighting for what we had, you were going to 'kick me to the curb' as one of our mutual acquaintances so casually put it not too long ago." There was a small pause where we both stood there breathing and looking at each other before I swallowed hard and said, "I think mine is the worst of our problems, so I'm sorry if you can't leave here feeling relieved and unburdened; however, I know you'll still be just fine."

"Tell me what I need to do," he urged. "I'll do anything, Selena, anything."

I looked at him pityingly. "I can't think of a single thing you can do, Tex. Just let it go."

He moved to me so quickly that my breath caught. He had my head in his hands. His thumbs caressed my jaw as he placed his forehead on mine. His eyes closed as mine did. I weakly brought my hands up to grab his wrists, intending to move him away from me. But my attempt was halfhearted, so they just held on to him as we breathed together.

"I'll find a way," he whispered, as he brought his lips to my forehead and kissed me there. "You may not be able to think of anything, but I will. By the grace of God, you are back here, in my sight, in my presence. I have waited so long. There is no way I am letting this slip through my fingers again. I don't care if it takes me another decade or a lifetime. I will do right by you."

He gently moved me to the chair and pulled tissues from the box on the table. He handed them to me, and I pressed them against my face as the tears I had so desperately tried to keep in check tumbled down my cheeks. Just after I wiped them away, I heard the door close, his car start, and finally the gravel as he backed out of the driveway and headed off down the road. I shook with fresh aches and tears.

nineteen

SO, THAT WENT WELL

Tex tossed his keys into the small glass bowl that sat atop the table in the foyer. When he finally got a place of his own, his mother insisted on being the one to decorate it, which ended up with him owning a lot of furniture he never would have thought to pick out for himself. It truly never would have crossed his mind to own a table that is solely decorative and creates a home for his key bowl.

The entire condo was decorated in plush whites and sleek blacks. The kitchen was awash in chrome. He let out a deep sigh as he trudged into the kitchen and grabbed a bottle of cold water from the gigantic fridge that only housed his bottled waters and pre-made meals from Gretchen, their trusted housekeeper, whom he'd known since he was six. She was a jack of all trades for their family. Housekeeper, chef, and nanny. She did it all.

He downed a large gulp of water before looking around with an irritated huff. His condo was bigger than my whole house.

Selena.

His eyes closed as his hands splayed on the kitchen

island before him. It was an absolute shock to see me after all these years. To be honest, he was a little glad I'd fainted. It gave him enough time to have his freefall into bewilderment before he was able to get it together and consider the best course of action when I finally fluttered my eyes open again.

The resounding clack of his shoes gave testament to their expense with every step to his bedroom. He undressed, showered, and prepared for bed with muscle memory as his thoughts fixated on the woman he'd loved since high school. I was here. He'd seen me, we had talked, and we'd even had dinner together. In his opinion, I was still the most beautiful girl he had ever seen, and even more so now that I was actually in womanhood. My hair was longer, and the relentless curls I battled daily were now somehow softer, falling perfectly around my face. The big brown eyes he's always loved were enticing before, but now with the light eyeliner I was rimming them with, they practically popped out and begged to be recognized, as was my body! He shook his head as he lay back on his king-sized bed, the white sheets and fluffy comforter bunching up.

His head crouched up a bit as he reached back and adjusted his pillows to support him better. My body was not something he needed to be focusing on right now, although he was finding it very hard not to. No, he needed to concentrate on where to go from here. He had royally screwed things up all those years ago by letting his father control every facet of his life back then. A long, deep sigh escaped him as he looked up at the ceiling. Moonlight played with the shimmer of the pearl-colored paint coating the entire area above him. A delicate scallop design swirled from the outer wall to the center, where a small but ornate chandelier hung delicately above. He knew he couldn't fully blame his father. The choices were always his to make. He had just been a selfish coward back then. Not now, though, not this time around. This time, he wasn't going to let anyone or anything stand in his way. With all his heart, he believed we were meant for each other; he had always known it. From the first time he saw me on that beach, he was already envisioning our lives together. Wedding, children — the whole deal was flashing before his eyes before he'd even held my hand that first night.

If only he had left as soon as his father's tirade concluded that prom night all those years ago. But he didn't. No, he was so mentally and physically exhausted that when he got to his room and found Vanessa there, he just didn't have any fight left in him. It was obvious what she'd wanted. When she finally left, he was already cutting it close to pick me up, and the guilt was already eating him alive. Thoughts of the argument he and T.C. had before he was bombarded by Vanessa played on an endless loop in his mind.

"You're not going to some stupid high school ritual, boy!" His dad had bellowed, all red-faced and spitting. "We've got too much riding on completing this deal. It's all hands on deck."

Tex had stomped for the door with a frustrated growl. "I already told you I couldn't cancel. The tickets are bought, the restaurant is reserved, and Selena is waiting for me!"

T.C.'s face had gone from a bright red to a deepened purple as he stepped closer, throwing out his meaty hand and pointing it in Tex's face as he spit out through clenching teeth about loyalty, responsibility, and ensuring that their legacy continued for future generations. He carried on about Tex being bred for success and social status, and rooting around with some gypsy would do nothing but taint the name he's worked so hard to preserve.

The fight continued for what seemed like hours, with the two of them going back and forth until Tex could no longer do it. He knew he was cutting into precious, needed time now, and it wouldn't stop until his father got his way. So, with all the hate he could muster, he caved and let his father win, agreeing to break my heart, no — not just my heart — he agreed to tear us both apart just to make his father happy and end this constant nightmare of being told night after night of his obligations.

Just a few hours after that, he had seen my face for the last time. Those beautiful eyes he raved about, quivering in anguish. I had seen Vanessa — I had seen everything; he knew it — and then I was gone. One moment it was as if the entire world was on pause, and the next I was a flash of pale yellow. He'd tried to get to me, tried to reach me, but it was to no avail.

The bed rustled as he turned on his side and pulled his phone off the nightstand. My eighteen-year-old face smiled back at him. Even though he'd dated other girls since then and had way too many one-night stands, he never once changed the wallpaper on his phone. It was always me, and it would always be me. He set his alarm, tossed the phone back on the stand, and rolled onto his back, sliding his strong arms behind his head. Nodding his head once, he determined that I would be his again. He refused to believe anything else.

twenty

IT'S NO BIG DEAL, RIGHT?

Though every bit of me wanted to call in sick the next day, I knew I couldn't. Darnell was expecting a report, and my future career was at stake. He received my first notes and was thrilled; he even commented on how I seemed to be able to get a deeper insight into a person just from a *Q&A*. I took the compliment; he didn't need to know where my deeper insight came from.

After that, I threw myself into my work to make sure my debut as a true journalist was perfect. The article launched in Sunday's edition, and I was free to think about things other than Texas Conrad. However, the banging on my door woke me from a peaceful sleep. The person didn't even ring the doorbell, just fist against the door. How rude!

"Alright," I complained, trudging to the door.

"Don't you take that tone with me, Selena Ayers!" Cassey barked from the other side of the door. "You have some explaining to do!"

"Yes, you do, Selena!"

The second voice was Amber's, and she sounded just as irritated as Cassey was. I figured it wouldn't be long after the article was published that they would be after me, but I had hoped to at least sleep until, like, eleven maybe. I braced for impact and opened the door.

"Care to explain this?" Cass snapped at me, shoving a copy of the paper in my face as she did.

"Good morning to you as well. Would you like to come in?" I asked, turning my back on them and heading to the kitchen. If I was going to be interrogated, I needed caffeine.

"Oh no, you don't, girlie," Amber told me, following in my wake. "We are your best friends, and we find out you not only saw your ex but actually sat down with him and gave an interview and didn't even hint to us about it!"

"It's no big deal," I said nonchalantly, looking back over my shoulder at them. It was evident that both of them wasted no time getting to my front door this morning. Cass was in black joggers and her favorite hoodie, proving she put no real thought into getting dressed. Amber did a little better with jeans and a t-shirt, but she'd just slipped into her sneakers without making sure she at least pulled on no-show socks. That was a personal pet peeve of hers to do such a thing.

"No big deal," Cass said, mimicking my voice. "Selena, this man did a number on you. Maybe I'm having a hallucination here or something, but I seem to recall lying, betrayal, and cheating. So bad, in fact, that you tucked your tail between your legs and took off from your family and friends. Doesn't that merit a shout-out to us when you realize you are going to have to be in his presence again?"

"I didn't realize it," I told them, grabbing a soda. "Darnell sent me off to interview one of the *big wigs*," I said, making air quotes as I did, "and it turned out that it happened to be Tex."

"Oh, Selena…" Amber cooed pityingly, "I am so sorry. That must have been excruciating for you."

They had both stopped after entering the kitchen, Cass leaning on the door frame while Amber held up the counter with her waist. She was small enough to have popped up on it, but we tease her too much about her little legs kicking when she does things like that.

"I fainted."

"What?" They both exclaimed. In different circumstances, the customary *"jinx, you owe me a coke"* mantra would have followed, but apparently this situation was too serious for that kind of behavior.

I nodded my head up and down while swallowing the soda. "Yep," I said, setting the bottle down. "He walked in; I saw him, and the next thing I knew, I was waking up on the couch in his office."

Both girls came over and wrapped me in a hug. They were treating me like an injured child and telling me they were so sorry. I laughed at their behavior, but I'll admit it felt kind of good to be comforted.

"Guys," I told them, "I'm fine now. Really. I mean, yes, it was a shock." I grabbed the soda and made my way to the living room to sit in a chair. They both took an end of the couch as I continued. "But I knew it was inevitable to see him eventually. Granted, I had hoped to handle the situation a little better."

"What has Ryan said about it?" Amber asked.

I choked a little on the soda I was drinking before wiping my mouth and answering. "Um, well, he hasn't said anything about it other than that I did a wonderful job on the article."

They were both staring daggers at me. I avoided their gaze.

"Selena," Cassey said, "tell me you have told Ryan all about Texas Conrad the Fourth."

"He knows about him."

"Other than what he read in your article?" Amber asked, crossing her arms over her chest and giving me a withering look.

"He may know more than what's in the article," I admitted, shrugging a shoulder.

"Are you kidding me?" Cassey exclaimed, leaning forward to look me in the face, "You haven't told him about you and Tex? He doesn't know anything?"

"Well, it's never come up," I defended, holding up my hands in a *what do you expect me to do* gesture. "Why would I want to go through all that? Ryan and I are great. He's so good to me, and we get along, and everything is great, so why would I want to drudge up the past for no reason?"

"Everything is great," Cassey smirked. "That's why you've never been intimate with him then, because everything is great, right?"

"Not every relationship moves at the speed of light, Cass."

"Most don't move at the speed of a snail either. It's been over six months!"

"We've not gotten to that point yet," I argued, narrowing my eyes on her.

"Bull!" She shot back, cocking an eyebrow in challenge to my glare.

I pushed my bottom back into the chair and threw up my hands. "Fine. Alright, fine. I know Ryan would like more. He doesn't force the issue or say anything, but I can see the disappointment on his face every time things are headed in that direction, and I say I need to leave or tell him I have a deadline to make." I blew a breath up my face, which made my hair shoot up and fall back down. "I don't know what's stopping me. I'm crazy about him, and it seems he feels the same about me."

"From what I can see, it certainly seems like Tex is the problem, not you," Amber concluded, picking non-existent lint off her jeans as she spoke.

"How is that?" I asked, certain my face was portraying the confusion I was feeling.

She leaned forward to match Cass and myself. "Because even though it's been all these years and you've managed to learn to function, you are still afraid of having to go through that again." She shrugged as if what she was saying made perfect sense. "It's obvious, isn't it? That's why you passed out when you saw him. You were doing well and making progress with Ryan, and you thought you would be able to keep making headway, but then Tex just showed up, right when you were getting it together, and that fear has risen to the surface once again." She then pushed her glasses back up her nose as she finished her speech. "He's the cause of your hesitancy with Ryan, and now he's going to cause you to pause for a possible happy future."

She crossed her arms smugly over her chest and raised one eyebrow. Truthfully, she was right, and that meant I was stuck. "Well, I'm open to suggestions," I told them, holding my hand open at one and then the other in turn. "What do I do about it?"

Cassey's hand shot out and snagged mine. "We got you, girl," she said, winking at me.

"Yeah," Amber agreed, throwing her hand in with our own.

We laughed together. The girls got up from the couch and flung themselves onto my chair. We were laughing and squishing each other. Both of them gave me advice and demanded that I contact them immediately if any future issues arise. As I waved and watched them drive off, I thanked God for my friends. They are such a blessing.

———

Remember when I told you that I snuck a peek at the calendar and found out that Tex would be at our Christmas function? You do? Well, at least one of us did. Because I sure didn't.

After Cass and Amber's intervention, I made up my mind to do better with Ryan. He was certainly doing right by me after all. When he made one of our dates a dinner and a movie at his house, I showed up and didn't leave until the next day.

I got up from his couch and stretched. I secretly envied him for this navy couch. It was one of those that you could move around and re-shape anytime you got bored of the setup. Right now, it was set out so that there was a longer section at the end where we lay together and cuddled. He stood up as well, turning off the television, before walking past me and out of the room. I went behind him, but when he headed to the door as he normally does to kiss me good-night, I turned right and headed for the stairs that led up to the two bedrooms and bathroom on the second floor. One room in particular was my destination.

"Selena?" he asked, "Uh, isn't it late?"

I stopped and turned to him, my hand resting on the banister. He was looking up at me, one hand resting on the doorknob, the other tucked into his pants. His eyes were curious as he took me in. I gave him an inviting smile. "Yes, it is. That's why I'm heading up to your bed."

"My bed?" he asked, still watching me curiously.

I let the grin slide further up my face and asked softly, "Is that a problem?"

He didn't need to be asked twice. "No ma'am." He assured me as he locked the door and took the steps behind me. When we were in the room, he grabbed my arms gently, turning me to face him. I was suddenly aware of how close his queen-sized bed was to me. I loved the bed because he had one of those awesome purple mattresses. I was with him when he bought it. He also let me pick out the red and gray comforter set it was currently swaddled in. Thoughts of the bed continued to skitter through my mind as he leveled his eyes on me.

"Selena I…" he took a deep breath and blew it out, bringing my hands up to his lips and kissing them. "I just want you to know that I am in love with you."

I started to speak, but he stopped me.

"No, just listen," he said, holding up a finger to my lips. "I know this is the first time I've told you, but I'm not saying it to you because of what might be about to happen. I want you to know that I love you *before* I tell you that if you are not comfortable, if you are not one hundred percent sure that you want to spend the night with me," he reached a hand out to caress my cheek, his eyes unable to hold my gaze as he spoke the next words, "I will still be yours tomorrow, and the day after that, as long as you'll have me."

I grabbed the hand that had been caressing my cheek. "That's good to know," I told him just before I kissed his hand and looked back up at him. Smiling slyly, I said, "By the way, I expect breakfast in the morning."

I felt his hand slightly twitch in my own. Keeping my eyes on his, I reached up with my left hand and shut off the light. I heard his breath hitch just as I brought my lips to his.

That was two weeks ago.

Tonight we are in our office building having our annual Christmas party. Ryan and I had just finished a dance when he went to get us drinks. I went over to the sofa-sitting area to take a break and talk to some office acquaintances. Cheryl, the plump lady with the graying raven hair and unfortunate mustache, beamed at me as I sat. She immediately began telling me about all the new goodies they would be getting for the building's cafeteria next year.

Up at the open bar, Ryan was ordering our drinks when Tex moved up beside him.

"Mr. James, how are you?" Tex asked him.

Ryan turned to him. "Mr. Conrad, I didn't know you were coming tonight."

"Harmon insisted, said it was quite a deal, and wouldn't have us missing it."

"Well," Ryan said just as he was given our drinks, "glad you could make it. Most of our clients do attend the party, but I would have thought that, um…"

"That our company's people were too rich and pretentious to mingle with the common folk?" Tex finished for him, laughing.

Ryan laughed as well and said, "I wouldn't have put it that way, but sort of, I guess."

"Hopefully, you will continue to find that we are just as down to earth and community-oriented as anyone else," Tex said, then noticing the drinks, he quickly added, "I'm sorry, you're here with someone, and I'm keeping you from them. I'll just…"

"It's alright," Ryan interjected. "I've just got us drinks. Come with me and I'll introduce her to you. She writes for the paper."

The two of them began making their way toward me, though I was none the wiser.

"She writes?" Tex asked, raising an eyebrow and keeping pace with Ryan. "Have I read any of her articles?"

Ryan laughed, "Actually, she's interviewed you personally," he said before calling out to me. "Babe, look who made it to our little gathering."

I turned to receive my drink and found Ryan and Tex standing side by side. I stood up quickly, looking from one to the other and smoothing down the short black cocktail dress I had chosen for the occasion. Forcing a smile, I took my drink from Ryan and thanked him. Ryan moved over to me, kissed me quickly, and then put his arm around my waist as he addressed Tex.

"She interviewed you as Sel Mayer, but she's actually…"

"Selena Ayers." Tex finished, keeping his eyes on me. He was dressed impeccably sharp in crisp black slacks and a designer silver and black pin-striped shirt. His cologne wafted over to me, and I took a drink to keep from inhaling too deeply.

"Yeah," Ryan told him, squinting a little in confusion. "Do you two already know each other?" he asked, moving a finger back and forth between us. "Other than the interview?"

I looked at Tex a moment more before turning to Ryan and saying, "We, um…"

"We went to school together," Tex said over my words. He then laughed a little and gave Ryan his attention. "Selena was at S.C.H.S. up to our senior year, but then she left close to graduation because…"

"My grandmother," I said, taking my turn to interrupt, "she needed me, and, in a way, I needed her." I gave Tex a leveling look before turning back to Ryan.

"Ah," Tex said, shoving his hands in his pockets, "your grandmother's. I wasn't quite sure where she lived."

"Well, it's not something one goes around talking about to just anyone." I offered, giggling and making a face as if what he'd said was absurd.

"Just anyone?" Tex asked, raising an eyebrow at me.

At this time, the DJ mercifully put on a slow song, to which I was able to excuse us from Tex and make Ryan take me to the dance floor. Every time Ryan tried to bring up Tex and our high school years together, I answered vaguely before changing the subject. For the first part of our dance, I was more than aware that Tex was staring at us from the bar. Then, with relief, I was happy to see that I couldn't find him anywhere.

We stayed another couple of hours before Ryan drove me home. Tomorrow was Christmas, and we had agreed to start with each of our families before coming together for the day. At the door, Ryan held me close and told me how he didn't want to leave. I giggled a lot as he nipped at my neck and ears. Finally, he gave me a long, lingering kiss before telling me good night and driving away.

I unlocked my door and walked inside. After locking up, I took off my shoes and placed the keys on the side table. I was still caught up in the bliss of the kiss as I made my way into the living room and flicked on the light. Then I screamed bloody murder!

twenty-one

THERE ARE BOUNDARIES, YOU KNOW!

"WHAT ARE YOU DOING IN MY LIVING ROOM?" I yelled when I finally gathered my senses.

Tex was standing by the window. I noticed he had taken his tie off and placed it on the couch. The top buttons on his fancy shirt were unbuttoned, and he looked a little disheveled. His hands were at his waist. This was not a good thing. Anytime Tex was truly ticked off, his hands went to his waist and took up residence. I swallowed but made myself stay fierce. He was in *my* home after all.

"So that's the reason why you haven't been returning any of my calls or emails, or allowing me to contact you except to thank you for the article." He accused, narrowing his eyes and coming around the coffee table as he spoke.

I groaned out loud, flung down my purse, and turned to stomp into the kitchen. I could hear Tex stomping after me.

"Do not turn your back on me, Selena. I want to talk to you."

"Apparently so," I snorted, "so much that you break into my home to do so!"

"I didn't break in," he informed me with that smug voice of his, "the spare key was in the fake rock by the steps, just like the one your parents have."

I mentally kicked myself. Honestly, in all my efforts to forget this man, I had made myself forget things that I needed to remember. Like how much he knew about me, for example.

Once in the kitchen, I made my way straight to the sink. I got a glass of water, took a long drink, and turned to see where he was. He had stopped only a few feet from me, his chest rising and falling as he waited for me to say something. His hands were still on his waist. I shook my head in irritation.

"He doesn't even know about me or about us, does he?" Tex asked. It was a rhetorical question because we both already knew the answer to that one.

"No," I admitted, leaning against the counter and holding the cold glass against my forehead for a moment of comfort.

"How long have you been seeing him?"

"Eight months."

Tex let out a whistle. "Eight months," he said, "that's a long time, Selena. Why haven't you told him about us?"

I lifted my head and looked at Tex. He had his head cocked to the side, awaiting my answer.

"Why should I?" I snapped at him. "You and I were years ago; we were young and in high school. Everyone has a boyfriend or girlfriend from their past. It's irrelevant."

"You know very well that you and I were more than just a typical high school relationship."

"Were we?" I asked hatefully. "Because no matter what it had seemed like to me, it obviously wasn't the same for you."

I pushed past him into the hall and stomped up the

stairs. My purpose was to shut him out somehow or find some way to discourage him from bothering me anymore. I made it into my room and turned; now he was in my bedroom doorway. I threw up my hands.

"Why are you here, Tex?" I asked, not even bothering to mask my frustration, "I mean, what do you want from me? You said you tried to find me, but you couldn't. You said you wanted forgiveness, and I told you it didn't matter. You see that I am in a relationship with someone else, I have a career, and I have moved on. You don't need to feel guilty. It's fine. I'm fine."

My chest was heaving. I had ended my rant with a little hysterical laughter of sorts, and even though I had said all of that, Tex still stood there, just watching me. He looked down for a moment, then removed his hands from his waist and leaned against my wardrobe. I watched him as he found interest in his fingers.

"Do you love him?"

The words breezed from his lips the way a leaf falls from a tree when summer is over. When I didn't answer, he looked at me and waited. I licked my lips and looked away. "I care so very much for Ryan," I told him. "He loves me, is a wonderful man, and…"

"You didn't answer the question."

"Everything about Ryan is perfect. He makes me feel good about myself and does everything he can to…"

"Answer the question!" he demanded.

"I AM ANSWERING THE QUESTION!" I yelled.

"YOU'RE AVOIDING IT!" he yelled back at me. We both stood there heaving, eyeing each other to see who would cave first. Swallowing hard, Tex slowly opened his palms and said, "Just tell me, Selena, do you love…"

"HE'LL NEVER HURT ME!" I screamed out at him,

throwing the stuffed pig from atop my bed at him as hard as I could.

Tex dodged the pig, then straightened and glared at me. I took two heavy breaths before closing my eyes and trying to compose myself enough to speak to this man without losing it entirely. Looking at him was not helping. I had to get some sort of control. My next words were barely more than a whisper.

"He will never betray me," I said, tears threatening to spill over my lids.

He stepped toward me then. I opened my eyes, but I didn't look at his face. Instead, I watched as he twisted his class ring around on his finger. "So," he said, "in other words, you are telling me he's *safe*?"

My strength was waning. I moved back to lean against the wall. "What do you want from me?" I begged him. "Are you just upset that I never actually gave you the chance to break my heart in your own way? I mean, since I know what your father expected of you and I actually saw your indiscretion with my own eyes, you couldn't sugarcoat it and make yourself feel better about what you were going to do to me, so now you want to figure out some way you can replay that night and not feel terrible about it or something?"

Tex walked closer to me. There were barely three feet between us now. He held out his hand to me. I gave him a quizzical look in return, eyeing his offered hand warily.

"Trust me," he said, "just come and sit down. I need to tell you something."

It took a beat, but I finally gave in and held out my hand to him, letting him lead me around in front of the corner chair.

"Sit down, Selena," he said, then politely added, "please."

I sat down. He moved over to my bed and sat on the end of it. It was quiet in the room as he picked up another one of my stuffed pigs and fidgeted with it. I waited patiently. Finally, he said, "Do you remember when things first started to mess up with us? When I came over to your house and just wanted to hold you?"

"I remember," I answered. In truth, it was a moment in time I can never seem to forget. It was what got the ball rolling down the hill of crap. Well, so to speak.

He nodded his head a couple of times. "That was one week after my father had brought Mr. Ewing to the house. At first, I thought Mother and I were just meeting new people—possible business partners—but after they left, Dad called me into his office. It was also the first time Vanessa was shoved back into my life."

My face involuntarily fell, and my jaw tightened at the mention of her name. It may be true that I couldn't blame her for everything, but I wasn't letting her off the hook either. She knew about me; there wasn't any way she couldn't have known.

Tex paused and pinched his nose between his eyes. "Father, as you know, was petrified that the new businesses wouldn't make it to the black in time."

"Tex," I interrupted, "I know all this. You told me all this before."

"Please," he said, "let me finish."

I bit my lip and leaned back in the chair. "Go on," I told him with a flourish of my wrist.

"Thank you," he said with a smirk as if he were trying not to laugh, but he composed himself and continued, "I know I told you father's plan for the merger, but what you don't know, or rather what you haven't been told, is everything that happened after I failed to find you that awful night."

"I don't want to hear…"

"Selena, you said you'd let me finish."

I shrugged my shoulders but closed my mouth all the same.

"After I saw your face through that window and after having miserably watched you drive away, knowing I had lost you, I finally snapped. What was going on between me and Vanessa, and what my father was doing finally just clicked." Tex stood up and started to pace. "I defied my father right then and left the house. It was like I knew, the whole time everything was going on I knew how messed up it all was, but it was as if this part of me was refusing to let me see what a despicable, cowardly jerk I was. Thinking about it now, Selena, it makes me sick. I was just as deluded and self-righteous as my father." He momentarily stopped pacing and looked at me, searching my face for any sign that what he said was registering. I merely lifted my eyebrows, silently agreeing with his concluded opinion of himself. "I searched for you." He continued, in words and in pacing. "I was out until the next morning before I finally came home. Mother and I talked for a long time, and she supported me completely when I told her I was going to do whatever it took to right this wrong. That support meant the world to me because if what I did went horribly wrong, she would be suffering the consequences right along with me."

I wasn't surprised that his mother supported him in making big decisions. She loves her son and anyone with eyes can see that. Now Tex was at the other end of my bed. He sat down again. "I arranged a meeting with Mr. Ewing that my father didn't know about. When I met with him, I poured my heart out and told him all about our need for this merger and how I wanted to do anything I could, whatever it would take to make the merger happen, but that I needed him to understand something."

"Is there a…"

"Selena…"

An exasperated sigh escaped me as I got up and went back to leaning against the wall. Tex stood up as well, watching me. Every part of me wanted to scream or bolt like I had all those years ago, but I reasoned that if I could get through this, if I could just let him have his say, then maybe it would be enough.

"I'm listening," I assured him, indicating that he should continue.

"Right, well, I told Ewing that I needed him to understand that I was in love with you, gypsy or not, or any other questionable background he might find a problem with," he said, and then he laughed a little. "Mr. Ewing looked shocked at first, but then the biggest, broadest smile lit up his face. He waggled a finger at me before sliding open his desk drawer and pulling out a small book. I was truly curious as I leaned over the desk to see what was on the pages."

"Well, what was on them?" I asked, annoyed that he was dragging this out.

"His grandson," he answered with a wide grin, "you see, even though his daughter knew how badly her father wanted to get into the oil and gas business, she fell in love and had a child with someone he once would have considered a problem. After that baby was born, though, things changed for Mr. Ewing. Through loving that child, he realized how antiquated and wrong his beliefs had been. He begged his daughter's forgiveness and has since become the best grandpa around." Tex paused for a beat, checking for my reaction. Since I was still wondering what any of this had to do with me, I just raised my eyebrows. A silent way of asking if there was more to the story. He cleared his throat and continued, "Anyway, the problem is, or was, my father. Just as my father thought he knew all he needed to know about Jackson Ewing, Mr. Ewing had done his research as well. He was trying to keep his grandson and son-in-law on the down low so that the news of them didn't ruin this possible merger because of my father's preju- dices." Tex laughed out loud here. "When I came to him with my news, he said it was a prayer answered. I knew how badly Father wanted the merger, so we called our lawyers, drew up the contracts, and signed the documents right then and there."

"And what about your father?" I asked hatefully. "Did he just magically decide not to be a bigot?"

Tex cocked his head and shook his finger as he said, "I walked into his office with the signed contract papers and tossed them on the desk. When he was grinning and looking them over, I informed him that his deal was done, and then I proceeded to tell him everything I had done, from searching for you to telling him everything I just told you about my meeting with Jack. The last thing I told him was that Vanessa and I were never, ever going to happen, and I didn't care what he did or said because there was no way I was ever going to so much as speak to her again, let alone marry her."

He moved over to my vanity and began fiddling with my lipstick as he finished his tale. I watched him take the lid off and twist the tube before twisting the caramel- colored tint back down again. He dropped the tube and turned, using his hands to balance as he leaned back onto the vanity wood. "He was furious, of course," Tex admit- ted, "but I stood my ground and told him I would never again allow his ridiculous notions and hateful ideals affect my life in any way, and the fact that he was my father was the only thing that kept me from shutting him out of my life completely. In his anger, he refused to help me find you, stating that while things may be good for business, he still believed I was too young and in over my head when it came to you. From that day on, Mother and I have barely spoken to him. They have basically lived apart, as mother stays on one side of the house and dad is either in his office, at the office, or staying in the beach house."

"Poor man," I said sarcastically.

Tex smirked. "Yes, well, lately we have noticed what seems to be a slight change in him. Ewing's little grandson is around the office a lot, and my father seems to actually enjoy his visits. I've noticed he has bought the boy a football and whatnot. In the past month, he has shown up at a couple of dinners. There isn't much conversation between the three of us, but it's the first time he's eaten at the table in years."

"Well," I said, walking past him to stand against the wardrobe this time. "You've told me everything, I suppose. So, what now? What do you want me to do with this information? Am I supposed to forgive you, as Jackson's own family apparently forgave him for his ignorance?"

"To be honest, Elizabeth never really let her husband know what her father was like. She had let her husband believe that she and her father weren't very close and that he pretty much ignored her and what she did up until she was pregnant and they eloped." He admitted.

"Well," I gaffed, amazed he hadn't zeroed in on the difference between their secret relationship and our very exposed one, "that explains a lot then."

He moved in front of me. "Yes," he agreed. "Since her husband had no clue just how deep her father's hatred had run, nothing kept him from fully accepting his apology for being so distant, and therefore they got their happily ever after."

"But I knew your father's hatred, Tex," I told him bitterly, fresh tears forming in my eyes, "and I heard you when you all but told me you agreed with him to end things with me. Oh, and let's not forget," I choked with a laugh, "you slept with someone else, and I saw you. I saw you, Tex, in the very bed where I gave myself to you."

I noticed he had moved closer to me. I stiffened a little. His eyes were haunted and searching mine. Looking away, I shifted so there wasn't anything against my back that would keep me from backing away or moving again.

"And it is this very thing that continues to destroy me day in and day out," he said, turning with me as I moved. "Every call you refuse, every message you decline…kills me. I've waited so long to see you again, and I was truly afraid I never would, but here you are. Goodness Selena, ever since you walked into my office, I have been trying to reach out to you to get you to just let me show you that I know I made a mistake and that I know I can't undo it, but I want to do right by you. I've been trying to make sure I was not being too pushy and understanding your feelings, but now I realize…"

"What?" I asked, truly curious as to what this epiphany is that he feels he's had, "What do you realize?"

"I realize that all my refused efforts are not because of your dismissal, but because of his presence."

My brows furrowed. "Ryan?"

Tex nodded.

I frowned at him. "Ryan has nothing to do with my feelings for you. I didn't even know him when you and I happened, and I didn't know him the years after. He has nothing to do with how much I can't stand you."

"He has everything to do with it," he countered, his

hands slowly inching toward his waist. "You admitted earlier that you aren't in love with him, but yet you stay with him. Now, why would someone do something like that? Unless they were still in love with someone else and were just too afraid to give them a second chance."

Now it was me who was getting angry, I stood up straighter and slashed my hand through the air as I forced out my next words. "My relationship with Ryan has absolutely nothing to do with you. I never said I didn't love him."

"You never said you did either."

"Regardless," I gaffed, "you don't get to come into my house after what you did to me and tell me how you can't understand why I won't have anything to do with you. What on God's green earth makes you think you deserve that privilege? I mean, are you kidding me? Why would I want to *EVER* give you another chance to do that to me again?"

"Because you still love me."

That did it. That flipped the switch. Forget moving on; forget the years, the past, and the possible future. I was eighteen again, and I had just seen this man begin dressing after breaking my heart into a million tiny pieces. All the rage, hurt, fury, pain, and disgust roared like a dragon from the depths of my soul. I flew at him, slinging my fists anywhere I could hit him and yelling like a banshee in the process.

"I HATE YOU!" I bellowed, "I hate everything about you. I hate that I ever met you on the beach." *Punch*. "I hate that I ever kissed your lips." *Slap*. "I hate that you ever touched me and made me fall in love with you." *Punch again*. "I hate that I made love to you and was so certain you'd be my forever!" I pushed him hard and moved to punch him again. "I hate that I saw you that day, saw her, and watched as she kissed your lips and you kissed her back, and I hate that you've hurt me and it still hurts!"

He easily swatted aside my final pushing attempts. The last was when he grabbed my arms and pulled me into him. I sobbed into his chest, reciting "*I hate you*" over and over again. He kissed the top of my head and held me tight, repeatedly apologizing for everything. When I could bear it no longer, I tried to shove away from him, but he snapped me back, pulling my wrists up between us and staring at my tear-soaked face.

"I love you, Selena. I have always loved you, and I will always love you. When I left your home the last time I was here, I told you I would find a way, and I meant it. I still mean it. I know you still love me."

"No, I don't." I argued, "I…"

But I didn't get to finish. In a swift motion, Tex slung me into him using the very wrists he had been holding. Our lips were together, and he was kissing me. I feebly punched at his arm, but he parted my lips, and the place I had holed up inside me opened, making me free-fall back into it.

There were frenzied hands, roaming lips, and tears. My body was on fire in ways that it had never been before. I was so enraptured by passion and hurt that I couldn't tell you how long these moments lasted. When all was said and done, I remembered one last kiss on my face and his whispered voice telling me that he loved me and that I would be his again. Another tear slid out of my eye as I drifted off into sleep, still wearing the dress I had worn to the party.

twenty-two

MY BIG BREAK... BUT THERE'S A CATCH

The next week at work was a blur. Tex had sent a bouquet of orchids with a note. When Ryan stopped in and saw them, I shamefully lied and said they were sent to properly thank me for writing such a great article. The note, however, said no such thing. The flowers were an apology for the anguish I felt the other night as well as a reminder of how much he knows and loves me. Orchids are my favorite.

I found out from Ryan that Generations Steel had hired their firm to represent them in the acquisition of more land needed for development. There has been a small issue in the community with some of the citizens, mostly tree-huggers protecting the earth at all costs, who felt that big business meant big environmental issues and the jobs weren't worth the cost to Mother Nature. Long story short, they were going to have to go to court and prove their business was more beneficial than harmful and convince the hippies that Mother Nature would prosper as well.

I half-listened to what he was telling me. I had become numb when it came to Tex. Thinking about him caused me pain. Not thinking about him caused me pain. I wanted to be in his arms, and I wanted to break his arms.

"And so then I just wore the dress because it did match my eyes," Ryan said.

"Yeah," I said, agreeing and stapling some pages together to send to editing.

Ryan laughed a little and sat at the edge of my desk. "I knew you weren't listening to me," he said, slapping my hand with the papers he was holding.

I came out of my reverie. "I'm sorry, what?"

He laughed again. "Did you not get enough sleep last night?"

"Not good sleep, I'm afraid."

Ryan smirked, then got up and walked over to me. He leaned down and nuzzled my neck.

"Maybe you should stay with me tonight. I can make sure you sleep well."

I squirmed a little as his breath tickled my neck. "I doubt I'd get any sleep at all," I quipped, turning to look at him.

There was a mischievous look in his eyes as he smiled. Goodness, he was gorgeous. What was wrong with me?

"AYERS!" Darnell barked from my doorway. "Quit canoodling and get in my office. I got big news."

"Yes, sir," I said, sighing and getting up from the chair.

Ryan slapped my rear with his papers and told me to get to it.

"I am. I am." I complained, as I headed out of the door.

Darnell was smoking a cigar at his desk. I knocked, and he growled at me to just get in the door already. I hurried inside and sat across from him.

"What's up?" I asked, smacking my hands together and leaning forward.

Darnell crushed his cigar, coughed a few times, and wiped his bushy mustache. "This is it, Ayers. It's the big deal. Your ship has come in, and it's a yacht."

"You've certainly got my attention."

"That industry chief you interviewed at the new steel plant. Tommy…"

"Texas."

"That's the one," he said, pointing a finger at me. "Turns out the company is having some difficulty with the local environment protectors. Gonna be a big case."

"I've heard," I admitted, "Ryan was just telling me the bits and pieces when you came by."

"Yeah, that's what it looked like," he said with a snort.

I narrowed my eyes on him. "Anyway," I diverted, "Generations is going to have a lawsuit. What does this have to do with me and my money ship?"

"*Our* money ship," Darnell corrected. "That interview you gave was a major success with these people. The head of the company, T.J."

"T.C."

"Yeah him," Darnell coughed again and fired up another stogie.

I waited for him to take a few puffs. He blew out the smoke and looked back at me. "He has personally requested that you cover the whole ordeal. They are going to give us one-on-one, upfront, and personal access to all the information. We will be the first paper with the goods, girlie. We get the exclusive. The pictures, the words, and most of all," he added, pointing his cigar at me, "the recognition."

My face lit up. This was big. Really big. Getting my name out there for this kind of coverage meant having true credentials. I could name my price after this. "Wonderful," I said, standing up. "I'll get in touch with their receptionist and work out a schedule to interview different department heads. After that, I'll go ahead and find out who the official land protection agency is going up against these guys. I'll probably be doing a lot of phone work and homework, but I'll keep you posted along the way."

"No, Ayers," Darnell ground out at me. "Sit down. We aren't finished yet."

I slowly sat back down in the chair and asked, "What do you mean?"

"I'm telling you that you were formally requested to be an 'on-site' reporter."

"On-site?" I asked, cocking my head to the side. "*Oh no, no he didn't,*" I was thinking. My palms began to sweat. It was suddenly very hot in here.

"That's right! They have made all the necessary arrangements for you. There is an estate down toward…"

"I know where it is," I said.

Darnell paused, looked at me quizzically, then went back to speaking. "Right, well, you will be there to cover the personal aspects of the case. The representatives are expected to spend practically every evening there, preparing for court. You will also be given a full-access security pass to the grounds. No area will be off-limits to you. When it's trial time, you will fly with the company and be put up by them in the same hotel. You will be fully provided for. All you need to do is show up, take notes, and write one heck of an article."

I was starting to suffocate. I stood up, placed my hands on top of my head, and paced back and forth, breathing slowly. Darnell watched me.

"Don't be so dramatic!" He demanded. "Yes, it's a big break, and we are all depending on you to pull this off so phenomenally that we can all be set for life in this little town, but you can handle the pressure."

"*Oh, if you only knew,*" I thought. I stopped and leaned against the door, sliding down to bend my knees a little and hold them while I took deep breaths.

"Ayers, you are not allowed to die on me. I'm counting on you."

I nodded my head up and down before making myself get up. I opened the door and looked back at Darnell. He watched me intently as I offered him a thumbs-up and a forced smile while sliding out the door.

Darnell eyed the door as my shadow passed. "That is the strangest girl," he grumbled, raising his eyebrows.

I went straight past my office and headed to the restroom. I don't know what I hoped to accomplish here— maybe a scream, a laugh, or a sobbing cry—but I burst in nonetheless. After pacing quickly back and forth several times, I made my way to the mirror over the sink. Placing my hands on either side, I took deep breaths and spoke to myself.

"You are fine," I said, "you are perfectly fine, and this will be fine. You are a professional. This is a job. It's just a job."

A toilet flushed, and the stall door at the far end of the room flew open. To my horror, Patty walked out.

"Nervous breakdown?" she asked me, walking to the other sink and mirror. "I wondered how long it would be before you lost it again."

I continued to stare at the mirror. "Patty," I said evenly, "it would be super great if you could just not talk to me for like… ever."

She laughed and turned to me, wiping her hands on the paper towel as she did. I begrudgingly had to acknowledge her presence, as it was evident she wasn't going to leave until I did. I gave her my most "*I hate you*" look.

She pouted out her lips like a baby. "Awe, poor Selena.

Maybe someday you'll be able to function like a normal person. Maybe." She shrugged her shoulders as she walked by me. "I doubt it," she added, opening the door. "But maybe."

The door swung closed. I stared after her, secretly willing her heel to snap as she made her way back downstairs. I didn't want her to die or anything, but if she could just fall like, I don't know, the last few stairs, that would be great. Just enough to lay her up in bed at home for half a year or more.

I turned on the faucet and let the water run into my hands. It was cool and felt good as I splashed it on my face. I would have to call Cass and Amber. They would raise all kinds of heck over this, but at least they could help me sort it out and come up with a plan of action. That's what I needed, my friends.

"It's not about him," Amber said, shoving a spoonful of ice cream into her mouth. We were at the DQ. She swallowed the bite and continued saying, "It's about the money. After everything he did to you and put you through, he owes you this break. You keep it professional and use him to make a name for yourself."

"That's good, and I like it," Cass agreed, pointing her spoon at Amber and nodding her head. She licked her lips, "But in keeping that energy and building on it. Once you have made that name for yourself, we use that security pass to get the jump on him when he least expects it. We hide in his office behind the door down low, then he comes in, shuts the door, and *BAM*! We each punch him full force in the balls."

Amber and I watched Cassey as she continued to nod

her head up and down while eating her ice cream. Eventually, she looked up and stopped with the spoon still in her mouth. Her eyebrows furrowed. "What?" she asked hatefully.

"Dear Lord," Amber breathed, casting her eyes skyward.

We both laughed as Cass continued to be affronted. "Screw you guys," she snapped. "My idea was just as good, *if not better*, than any of yours."

"Awe, Cass," we cooed at her, "it is a good idea, it is." We both said, patting her arm and head.

"Dang right, it is," she claimed, wiping her face and hands with a white crinkly napkin. "You ladies are too soft."

Our laughter rang out into the DB. The workers have changed over the years, but our presence in the corner booth never will.

twenty-three

LET THE AWKWARDNESS BEGIN

Tex was pacing the living room at his parent's estate. He knew I was set to arrive anytime between five and six for dinner with everyone before the first official meeting of lawyers and clients. He'd barely been able to focus on business after kissing me the way he had that evening. Goodness, it took everything in him not to rip that dress from my body and have his way with me right then and there. He sighed for the fifteenth time in less than ten minutes. If he had done that, then things would definitely have gone to the crap house. I would probably have felt guilty and shunned him because of my relationship with Ryan, and even though Tex would have felt a little sorry for Ryan, he admittedly liked the man, he wouldn't have felt sorry enough to have regretted his actions. As far as Tex was concerned, I still belonged to him.

"Texas darlin', please come and sit down," his mother implored as she moved to where he stood.

Obediently, Texas followed and sat on the sofa with her. Probably a few minutes went by before he was up and pacing again. His mother sighed.

"It's not like this is the first time you're seeing her, dear," she called out to him.

"I know that, Mother, but it is the first time she's been here since everything happened. She's going to pull up into that driveway where…" he choked up, unable to say more. He just stood with his arms crossed over his chest, one hand holding his mouth as he stared out the window.

"Sweetheart, a lot of time has passed since then. She is a grown woman now and has even done quite well for herself, as I understand it. I think she'll be able to come here with her head held high and do the job she's supposed to do."

"But I don't want her to just do the job she's supposed to do," he bit out, starting to pace again. "I mean, I want her to do well, of course," he admitted, turning to look at his mother on the sofa, "but I also want to hope that the time we get to spend together will make a difference."

The sound of my car pulling up the driveway made him stop short. His mom watched as he flicked his head up and whitened. She breathed hard and gave an exasperated roll of her eyes as she rose from the sofa. "I'll get the door," she called back to him.

I had turned around twice before I finally made myself stay the course and make it to the estate. As it loomed into view, I had an unearthly flash of a young eighteen-year-old me in a pale yellow dress flying from the stairs, across the porch, and disappearing into the shadows. What on earth was I doing back here?

I parked the car and held tightly to the wheel with my eyes closed. *"Alright girl. You got this."* I willed myself. *"Just go in there, have dinner, take your notes during the meeting, and then you can leave. It's just a job. It's just a job."*

Tap. Tap. Tap.

I jerked and cried out. Tex's mother, who was smiling

brightly at me from outside the passenger window, spoke up, "Well, hey, sugar," she said sweetly. "I didn't mean to frighten you. You'd been sitting here for a minute, and I just wanted to check that you were alright."

I forced a smile and opened the door. "I'm fine. I'm alright." I protested a little too enthusiastically. "I was just um, just going over a few notes. You know, making sure I have the right mind frame for the evening."

"Right," she said, maintaining that smile. I'm sure she knew I was full of it, but thankfully she didn't call me on it. Instead, she wove my arm through hers and led me up to the door.

I noticed there were two other men in the entryway with her husband, T.C. and I momentarily stiffened, but she held my arm tight and spoke under her breath to me. The smile was still plastered on her face.

"Just hold the smile and breathe, darlin'," she told me.

I took her advice and plastered an equally fake smile on my face as we entered the room. T.C. gave me a curt nod as well as the other men. Tex came into the room a beat later and stood to his mother's right. I offered him a smile before looking away. His father was introducing the other two men, one of whom was Patty's husband, Mr. Garfield Harmon. I politely held out my hand and let myself be introduced. I was vaguely aware that Tex hadn't stopped staring at me from the moment he walked into the room. I was wearing a crisp white blouse with the neck open, a navy pencil skirt, and matching heels. My hair was pulled up, and loose curls hung from it.

"Texas, dear," his mother said.

"Hmmm?" Tex responded, still watching me.

"Your father has suggested we go in to eat."

Texas looked at his mother first and then back at the others who were watching him. He reacted immediately.

"Right," he said, clapping his hands together. "Let's go into the dining room then. Jackson will be a little late, but he will be here."

Everyone turned to go in, myself included. Hanging back a bit, his mother spoke to him quietly.

"Try to be less obvious next time, won't you?" she asked comically.

"I hadn't meant to be obvious then," he retorted in a fierce whisper.

I heard her laughing from behind me and blushed.

During dinner, I sat beside Mrs. Conrad, which was perfect for me as I had nothing to say to anyone else in the room. Tex kept trying to offer me things or ask me how I was doing. After the fifth time of me telling him I was fine, I saw him wince and reach down to his leg. He shot a look at his mother, who feigned innocence, and started a conversation with me about my grandma Pearl. I suppressed a laugh, and told her all about our family history.

After dinner, the action took place. Mr. Harmon and T.C. set to work with files and articles strewn across the table. There were land surveys and other court documents as well. I had to pull each one over to peruse and note. It was both a blessing and a curse. The blessing was in the fact that everyone was so caught up in the aspects of the case that there was no room for any other talk. The curse was in the fact that by the time I went back out to my car, Tex was lugging a box of copied files for me to use in my notes.

I opened the trunk, and he placed the box inside. "Thank you," I told him, moving to the driver's side door.

"You're leaving now?" he asked me.

I looked around. "Well yeah, we are through for the night. Aren't we?"

"For the case? Yes, we are finished with the case for tonight."

"Okay." I said slowly, not sure what he was getting at. "Then I'm going to head on out. It's late, and I still have to go through these files and type the first notes for Darnell."

"I could help you. Why don't you come up to my side and we'll get a snack, sit at the table, and get it together?"

My palms started to itch. I opened the car door and tossed my purse onto the seat. "Tex, don't you think…"

"Don't ask me what I think, Selena," he said quickly, "you'll get more information than you want." He reached over and closed my door. "Come on. I promise I'll behave. We'll just have a snack and get your first notes together, that's all."

You know I gave in. You knew I was going to cave before you even read these lines. I mentioned before that I am often non-confrontational and, well, now you know that's true. The good news is that he was true to his word. We ate chips and salsa while he kept his distance and helped me type through the first notes. Since he knew the information I needed, there wasn't any real need for me to scrutinize every piece of paper I had gathered.

"You know," I told him after swallowing a chip. "You are really smart. I remember you always doing well in school and football, but I just realized how in tune you are with all this."

"Thank you," he said.

He was going to say more when my phone rang, and Ryan's face appeared on the screen. I wiped my hand and grabbed the phone, sliding to answer.

"Hey," I said.

Tex stood up and started clearing away our mess as we talked. "Yes," I said to Ryan. "I'm on my way now. No, no, that's fine. You know where the key is. Alright, okay, see you in a bit."

I hung up the phone and raised myself to help clean. Tex moved around me and helped me close up the chips and wipe the table. I thanked him before heading to the door.

"Stay here," he said.

I stopped abruptly. "What? Why?"

"Because I know he is at your home and it's already eleven at night, which means he has no intentions of going to his own home," Tex said, his hands making their way to his waist. "*Oh boy*," I thought.

"Yes, he is at my home, but that doesn't mean he will stay all night and…" I realized I was explaining myself to him and became irritated. "And why am I telling you this anyway? Ryan is none of your business, as we already established."

I turned the knob and started down the stairs. Tex was thumping down each stair behind me.

"Presumptuous of him to just assume you would even be in the mood for company. You have been working all night, you know?" he reminded me angrily.

I barked out laughter. "Are you kidding me right now? You weren't too worried about my rest two hours ago when you offered snacks and more work."

"That was different. You were going to be working at home anyway. I was offering help."

"Well, maybe he wants to help, too," I spat, reaching for my car and pulling open the door.

"No, he doesn't, and besides, you don't need it. I've helped you. So you should just call him and tell him it's late and you'll see him tomorrow."

"I know we've got this messed up ordeal going on here, and things have gotten a little," I huffed, slinging my purse into the passenger seat, "well, things got out of hand, and I don't want to hurt Ryan, so with that being said, we are not having this conversation anymore."

"Oh, yes, we are."

"No! We are not," I said, cutting my hand across the air. "Goodnight, Texas. It is *you* that I will see tomorrow. Thank you for your help tonight." I got in the seat and shut the door. When I was putting on my seatbelt, I could see him reflected in my window. His tie was off, his shirt was unbuttoned at the top, and his hands were firmly at his hips. Yep, he was mad. I looked up at him.

"Send him home," he demanded.

I pretended I couldn't hear him as I waved and mouthed goodbye while driving away. Behind me, Tex's jaw grinded in anger. He turned fiercely and stomped back up the steps. "She's not going to send him home!" he swore at himself and slammed the door.

And so it went, day in and day out. I worked alongside the Generations' top men, doing everything I could to make sure I was reporting in-depth coverage for our readers. Most days, Tex and I were able to work together and call it a night, but other days, he insisted I talk to him or followed me to the car. There was even a time or two that he followed me all the way home. On these occasions, there was yelling, accusations, and a lot of tears. But I was proud of myself. I didn't give in to him or allow him to worm his way back into my heart again. At least I could brag about that, for a little while anyway.

twenty-four

DO I HEAR WEDDING BELLS?

Spring was here in no time. The weather was becoming more and more pleasant, and it looked like Generations Steel was on course to win their case. They were very conscientious of the surrounding environment and the community. We had been so busy, and time had moved so quickly, that I was unfortunately neglecting Ryan. I knew he was missing me, so when he asked me to set aside an evening for us, I readily agreed.

"You can't take the day off," Tex told me, "we are swamped with getting ready to go to Dallas, and I need you here."

I had just finished up at the estate and was walking toward the door. My strappy heels in the same maroon as my knee-length dress clicked with each step I took. My head turned back as I spoke over my shoulder to him, "Texas, we've talked about this. You are not my boss. Darnell is. That being said, you do not get to tell me what I can or can't do. Yes, you are giving me an exclusive, and I am grateful. But I do not have any bearing on your case whatsoever. I am just reporting from the field. I've already spoken with Mr. Harmon and Mr. Ewing, assuring them that I will meticulously pour over any notes that I miss."

My hand was on the doorknob. I turned and pulled the door open, just to have Tex reach out and close it again.

"Can we not do this, please?" I asked him, reaching my hand out for the knob again.

"Ryan James sees you plenty enough. You are working hard here. Doesn't he respect that?" he asked me.

"Really, Tex? Are you seriously going to play that card?" I shook my head at him and said, "Ryan has taken whatever time I have been able to give him and not once complained. He asked me to please make this time for him, and to be honest, he deserves it. He is my boyfriend, you know."

"Temporarily," he said.

"Don't start that again," I told him, turning the knob and flinging the door open.

He moved out onto the porch behind me but, thankfully, did not follow me to my car this time.

"Fine. That's fine, Selena. Go ahead and have your date with him. Just remember to be packed and ready to go in the morning."

"Will do," I called out, waving as I got into the car.

Ryan told me my dad wanted him to stop by to help with the baseball draft. That's my dad, from one sport to the next. Since he needed to see him, I just had Ryan pick me up there. Mom and I enjoyed spending time together upstairs as I used her vanity to put my makeup on and get ready. She fawned over Ryan and told me how lucky I was to have found such a good man. When she asked me how things were going with the job and Tex, I forced a smile at her. With a smirk, she kissed me on the head and hugged me tight.

"I'm always here for you, baby girl. You know I'm team Selena, no matter the outcome."

I nodded my head against her and hugged her back hard.

"Hurry up," she told me as she went out the door and down the stairs.

Dad gave a victory shout, so I gathered that he and Ryan had, once again, managed to do some good work when it came to the fantasy team. I finished up my primping and grabbed my things, noticing it was suddenly unusually quiet downstairs.

I went to the landing and called down, then moved from step to step until I could bend down and see into the living room. Ryan was there with my parents standing in front of my dad's overstuffed recliner, and they were all grinning at each other in such a way that it made me suspicious. I walked the rest of the way down loudly and stepped into the room.

"What's going on?" I asked.

Mother took her eyes away from Ryan and spoke a little too enthusiastically, "Nothing, hon. Just chit-chatting."

"Uh-huh," I said, looking at Dad and Ryan.

"You look beautiful," Ryan said, reaching out to kiss my cheek.

I moved my face up to assist him but kept my eyes on my parents, who were still just standing there smiling ridiculously.

"You two alright?" I asked them.

"Well, of course," Dad balked at me. "Now you two get going before it gets too late."

Ryan told them both goodnight and held my hand as he led me to the door. I gave my parents a sly grin.

"You two haven't been smoking that years-old pot that was hidden in the old Monopoly game, have you? You know you can't keep that stuff forever."

My mother's mouth dropped, and my dad laughed. "Selena Marie Ayers!" my mother said briskly. "No, we have not, and just how do *you* know about it at all, young lady?"

I laughed back at her. "You guys really should have found other places to hide the Christmas presents besides your bedroom closet."

"You little sneak," she said, pointing at me, "I ought to whoop your fanny for that. If you weren't grown, I swear I would."

"I know you would," I laughed at her. "I love you both. Goodnight."

"Yeah, goodnight, girlie. We'll talk again soon." Mom promised.

I was still laughing as Ryan led me to the car and helped me inside. "You are in trouble," he sang at me. This made me laugh that much more.

For the past few months, we've had to keep our dates local due to me not having time to do much else. Tonight was going to be special since Ryan had driven out of town and the city was coming up over the horizon.

"Where are we going?" I asked him.

"I've got a great night planned," he told me, bringing my hand up to his mouth to kiss, "since I finally get more than a few hours with you."

"I'm sorry I've had to work so much."

"Don't do that. You know I'm alright with it. I've certainly had to put my time in too." He turned the wheel, and we exited off the lighted bridge and onto Center Street. "I had hoped I would get to do some of the leg work with the firm out at the estate, but Harmon insisted they needed me back at the office dealing with the other clients and getting needed files out to them."

"Really? I didn't know that," I said.

"Yep, but it's alright. You are all mine tonight."

He smiled over at me, and I smiled back. No matter what, I was going to make sure he had a wonderful night out. One because he was so good to me, and two because I was all but certain that Texas Conrad had a lot to do with Mr. Harmon insisting Ryan stay at the firm. Just wait until I see him again.

As I noticed the city lights sparkling brightly in the distance, I became a little more excited for my surprise. Ryan took us to the same restaurant where we had our first date. We got the same table and reminisced about that night. He confessed how nervous he was and how much he hoped I liked Italian food. After dinner, he drove me out to the pier, and we repeated our first date by going down the boardwalk and visiting the same shops. When we were walking back on the beach, shoes in hand and surf lapping at our feet, I tugged his hand and looked up at him.

"Thank you for this trip down memory lane," I told him.

"It's not over yet," he said, and I realized we were at the same spot where he first kissed me. I laughed a little as he moved behind me and held me again. He hugged me close and kissed my head. We looked out at the ocean together, and I sighed, grateful for him and this time together.

Finally, just as before, Ryan slid around to my side, and I turned to face him. His hands cupped my face, and his lips fell onto mine. We had sweet little kisses and full-on passionate ones. When we stopped, I kissed him once more and squeezed his hand, turning to walk back to the car. Ryan's hand held mine, and he gently pulled me back to him. He was staring into my eyes, watching me as I came back to where I had been.

"What's wrong?" I asked him, searching his eyes.

"Not a single thing," he said softly. "Everything is perfect. I knew when I first met you that I had to do whatever I could to get you into my life. Over the past year, I have been so blessed. I'm a partner at my firm and our parents adore both of us. You are the love of my life. There is nothing left for me to accomplish except to move forward."

"Ryan, I don't understand."

But then I did understand. Right at that moment, Ryan slowly went down on one knee, which made me cringe a little thinking about the sand ruining those nice black slacks, but those thoughts were quickly shoved away as I watched him pull a black velvet box from his pocket. He lifted the lid and held it up before grabbing my hand again.

"I love you, Selena. There is nothing more I want in this world right now than for you to agree to spend the rest of our lives together. Will you marry me?"

Okay, so before I let you know how this scenario played out, let me first clue you into the inner workings of my brain. Did you ever see that one cartoon where the guy was to become a waiter who only knew fine dining? You know, the one where the boss tells him to empty his mind of everything except what he needs to be a great waiter? Well, the guy does it, but the problem is he'd done it so well that when he was asked his name he hadn't a clue what it was because he dumped that with all the other information he wouldn't need. I was that cartoon guy at that moment. All my brain Selenas were suddenly running around, pulling at different cerebral membranes, trying to get my thoughts to catch up to my mouth.

Ryan was still staring up at me. "Selena?"

"Yeah," I said, watching him.

"Is everything alright?"

"Uh-huh," I answered.

Ryan laughed. "Well then, do you think you could answer me?"

"Yeah."

He laughed again. "Yeah, you could answer me, or yeah to the question?"

I just nodded. Giggling to himself, he closed the box so he could grab my other hand, gently pulling me down to my knees in front of him. Well, this dress is ruined. I liked it a lot, too. Maybe I can get it dry-cleaned. A huff of breath slid out as I forced myself to concentrate on the moment going on before me. I closed my eyes as he brushed the hair out of my face and opened them to find him staring at me.

"You are so beautiful," he told me.

The next moment, he was kissing me as he had that first time so long ago. I felt the heat rush through me, and the tingles erupted up and down my arms. Why was I even confused? This man was the one who made me feel things I feared I would never feel again. He has loved me and been there for me all the time I was building myself up again. I would be crazy not to marry him.

"Yes," I said against his lips.

He slowly pulled back from me. "Yes?" he asked me, making sure I was looking right back at him.

I smiled, and it was the biggest, most genuine smile I could give. "Yes, Ryan James, I will marry you."

He tackled me after that, covering me as my back landed on the beach. We laughed and kissed for quite some time before he raised me back up to slip the diamond ring on my finger.

That night, I called my mother as soon as I could, and

she answered on the first ring. I knew they had been up to something.

"Yes, dear, is everything alright?" she asked innocently.

"Oh, don't play with me. You knew exactly what was happening tonight."

I heard her squeal and then heard my dad ask her what I'd said.

"I said yes," I told her, and then she excitedly told Dad, and they each tried to talk over each other on the phone.

After a bit, I told them I had to go and called both Cassey and Amber. It was late, but I told them they had to come to my house. When they both showed up, their faces looked as if they were ready to go to war. They probably thought I was in a fit with Tex again, but as soon as they started with angry words, I simply held up my hand, flashing the diamond ring as Ryan came to my side.

It was an outright scream fest. We all stayed up and talked for another couple of hours before the girls had to leave. Once the door was closed, I squealed out as Ryan scooped me up into his arms and carried me up the stairs. It was the most wonderful night.

twenty-five
FEELING GUILTY

Here is where you get to think badly of me, and I accept it completely. Before I left to board the plane with Tex, I removed the ring from my finger and put it in my jewelry tin. I know, I know, such a shady thing to do, but I just didn't want the drama. I especially didn't want it all the way in Dallas, and far away from any safe zones I could escape to. At the time, I was certainly glad I did, since Tex was determined to stick to me like glue. The company had a private jet, so we were to be taking off at seven on Monday morning. I took a seat by the window, opened my laptop, and set to typing. I was jostled by Tex sitting beside me. He was grinning and offered me Starbucks. I took it, eyeing him suspiciously.

"You're chipper this morning," I told him, taking a sip and being grateful that he remembered I hated coffee and got me hot chocolate.

"Yes, well, there's just something about knowing the woman you love isn't being fondled by another for at least the next two weeks that makes a man happy."

I choked on my chocolate, almost spitting the hot liquid

onto my favorite cream-colored slacks. "Really, Tex?" I asked, wiping a napkin across my face while giving him an evil look.

"Alright there?" he asked in retort, still grinning stupidly.

We had made it to Fort Worth International Airport and were off to the hotel in record time, and I was grateful for my suite. Well, honestly, I was absolutely in awe of my room. The entire suit was the size of my house. The carpets were soft plush white, which my feet sank into as I walked further in. The room opened up into a lavish sitting area with an L-shaped couch and sofa in the same soft white as the carpet, holding accented pillows in a wine-red color. A glass-covered coffee table was bearing a huge basket of fruit, flowers, champagne, and sweets that took up the majority of the space, with just a single rose vase behind it. A fireplace was built into the far wall, with a huge flat-screen television looming above it. A feeling of serenity washed over me as I watched the long, sheer white curtains flutter away from the insanely large glass windows. A small step up to my left led to a luxuriously enormous bed drenched in downy white blankets and more of those small wine-red pillows. The door to the left of the bed opened up into a bathroom that held a glassed-in standing shower, a jacuzzi tub, and a double sink with a mirror that took up the entire length of the wall. For all the white in the adjoining room, the bathroom was all black and chrome, with only a fluffy white rug in front of the sink to give a nod to the design as a whole. I was giggling like a teenager as I stepped to the other side of the bed and explored the walk-in closet. Once I had completely unpacked, there was still enough space in there for another three people's worth of clothes and accessories.

Aside from the suite, I was even more grateful for the fact

that Tex was focused on the upcoming case. When we met up in the hotel conference room to go over strategies and previous statements, which I was able to help with because I had been there for the majority of the sessions, he was all business.

We wouldn't be heading to court until the next day, so when the rest of the team showed up around five, we were fed and worked into the night. I was so exhausted that I didn't even protest when Tex insisted on seeing me up to my room.

It was a sensational week. There were flashes of pictures being taken every time we entered or exited the building. Several times I had to show off my press badge to the next eager beaver trying to cut in for a scoop. The majority of my answers were things like, "*No, I do not work for Generations Steel.*" Or "*Because I am from Saint Caine and was given the exclusive for our town.*" That one always awarded me a dirty look. The worst one to give was, "*Not a couple, thank you, just working together for the benefit of Saint Caine.*"

As I answered, Tex would just grin widely and wink at whoever was asking the question. This made it seem like I was "*protesting too much*" so to speak, and I even had to field calls from Ryan the next day as tabloids hit the stands.

"What would make them even think this?" Ryan asked heatedly.

I could tell he was pacing the floor as he spoke. I sighed into the phone.

"Who knows? It's not like it takes much. The reporters here are sensationalists."

"Yes, but the story is about the company and the lawsuit, not the individual personal relationships. The next time someone dares to ask you that, I want you to wave your ring in their face and tell them you are happily taken by Ryan James!"

I could practically see Ryan in his office right now. Standing behind his desk with his tie undone and his hair mussed from running his hand through it in aggravation. I smiled at the phone. "I will certainly do as you ask, Mr. James."

"I appreciate it, Mrs. James."

"Don't we have to wait until the end of August for that?" I asked teasingly.

"Not as far as I'm concerned," he stated.

I had managed to make it into the second week before Tex spoke of more than the case. It was my stupidity, honestly. I had been in a little spat with Ryan over the tabloids just minutes earlier and was still hashing over what was said in my mind. I was so caught up with filing through papers and thinking of "what I should have said" when Tex asked for the accounts of environmental protection performed by Texacon and Generations Steel that I, without thinking, sifted through the pile, found the piece, and handed it to him while barking, "They were right in front of you, Ryan!"

I whipped my head around in irritation, then widened my eyes into realization as I noticed Tex's jaw tightening. My last few words played over in my head. *"Oh no,"* I thought as I closed my eyes.

"Care to explain?" he asked.

I felt like a child who had gotten caught doing something bad. My ears were starting to burn, and I could feel that scared anticipation coming. Like when you just knew you were going to get the whoopin' of your life. I took a deep breath and looked around the room. I don't even know what I was looking for. I was just hoping for a miracle or for someone to need him for something.

"Selena," he said dangerously.

"Give me a second," I demanded, wringing my hands together. Finally, I decided to just come out with it.

"Just before we started going through all this, this mess," I blurted, indicating the mountains of papers before us. "Ryan called all upset over the latest tabloid. There is a picture of you and me going into the courtroom."

"So, there have been lots of pictures of you and me together since the start of this case. Why would that cause a problem?" He asked, and to my surprise he did seem as if he was actually confused.

I narrowed my eyes on him. "Because, Texas, in this particular photo, your hand is on the small of my back, just above my backside."

Tex's left eyebrow twitched up just briefly, and the corner of his mouth twitched a little. I gave him a scathing look.

"This isn't funny!" I snarled. The emotions and confusion wreaking havoc internally were starting to affect me externally. It is one thing to say pleasing things to others, but quite another to lie to oneself.

I looked down. Tex's hand caught my chin and lifted my face back up to his. I did my best to avoid his gaze. Why couldn't I have just paid better attention? He held my face there, clenching and unclenching his jaw as he looked at me.

"Please don't?" I whispered.

His look softened, and he let out a breath. "It doesn't matter," he told me, and before I could protest, he placed a finger on my lips and said, "I don't mean it's not important to you. I'm saying it doesn't matter, indicating that the guy is clearly in love with you and is acting out of jealousy. He just wants reassurance, which I assume you have adequately done. So, as I said before, it doesn't matter. He'll get through it."

Leaning in gently, he kissed my temple as he rose from his seat. With a squeeze on my shoulder, his hand slid off me, and I heard him walk out of the room. I closed my eyes and wondered why things couldn't ever just be easy.

There was a mandatory dinner the night before the final hearing. Everyone met in the hotel restaurant. As it was a very posh place, I made sure to look my part. There had been a burgundy satin dress in the window of a nearby store. I wasn't feeling like playing dress up through a closet of clothes, so I walked in, grabbed the dress, paid for it, and walked back out. Done and done!

Later that evening, I was walked over to our table by the hostess to be seated next to Mrs. Conrad, who happened to be on the other side of Tex. He immediately stood up, as did the other men, and pulled out my chair. As he pushed me forward he leaned down to my ear and whispered, "You look stunning, Selena. So beautiful."

I blushed and thanked him. This dinner went the same as any of the others. Mrs. Conrad and I spoke mostly to each other, and the men congratulated themselves on being so awesome. Dessert was winding down, and final drinks were distributed. There was an associate in attendance from Generations by the name of Mr. Van Hoffman. He was very rich and, equally, very old. His son was Magnus Van Hoffman, and he sat to his father's right. You could tell they were close. The elder Van Hoffman, Edgar, addressed Texas from across the table as he puffed away on an expensive cigar.

"Tell me, young man," he said to him, "why is it that you haven't taken this beauty beside you and left our company ages ago?"

T.C. sat back and watched the events unfold. Throughout our entire time together these past months, Tex's father and I had barely spoke more than three words at a time to one another. I did his interview by emailing my questions to his secretary, who, in turn, asked him and recorded his answers while he was in the middle of a shave and haircut. He looked at me momentarily before lighting his cigar.

Texas took a drink of his water before answering. "That is a very good question, Mr. Van Hoffman."

"Bah," Van Hoffman said, "Edgar, if you please."

Edgar gave me a wink, to which I returned a smile. He once told me that he has lived so long and will continue to do so for two reasons. The first was that he had so much more he wanted to accomplish before checking out of this life. The other, he told me as he jabbed an elbow into his son, was because he just wanted to hang in there knowing Magnus couldn't wait for him to pass the reins."

Magnus had replied by acting shocked and demanding that his father tell me that it was not a bit true. They shared a laugh between them, and it was quite endearing when Edgar clasped his hand on Magnus' neck and told him he was a good lad.

"Edgar," Tex said, addressing him respectfully, "the answer to that question is... well, complicated."

"You're young and foolish. That's why it's complicated. When you get to my age, you will learn to not hesitate when it comes to a woman such as her."

"Believe me, sir, it's not because..."

"I know this much," Magnus said as he leaned forward to light yet another cigar for his father. "If you don't intend to ask the lady out for the evening, I'm setting my mind to."

There was laughter across the table. I blushed profusely. "Well, I'm flattered," I admitted.

"Boy," Edgar told him, "must we tell you twice?"

"As I was saying, or trying to say, um, it's not that I have no desire. It's more a matter of my having to make up for past wrongs. I'm determined not to make the mistakes I have made before. There was a young lady that I had the pleasure of meeting on a beach when I moved to Saint Caine. It was only our junior year of high school, but I knew — I just *knew* she was going to be mine forever."

I coughed and leaned forward, grabbing my water for a drink. How on earth was I going to get out of this? Tex's mother reached over and squeezed my hand. I looked at her to find her giving me a *"hang in there"* look. I offered her a slight nod.

"We had the best time together," Tex continued. "I could stare at her for hours. Her laugh was infectious, and she did all she could to make me happy," he raised his eyebrows and held out his hands. "But I managed to screw that up and ruin everything I had been determined to build."

"So, you messed up with that one. Learn from your mistakes and try to make a go of it with the young lady beside you, assuming she'd want to waste her time with you, of course."

Laughter again. I noticed Tex's father had suddenly become very interested in his cigar. It figures he wouldn't dare chime in on this conversation.

"I couldn't blame her for not wanting to, that's for sure," Tex admitted, as he leaned back in his seat and folded his hands in front of him. "But I am determined to get back what I've lost. I know I don't deserve her. That's why once I finally have her again, I will never, under any circumstances, make the mistake of letting her go."

The men nodded to Tex and wished him the best of luck in getting this lady to forgive him for all his indiscretions. Magnus finished his drink and rose, coming around the table to us.

"That would mean this one is free for a dance," he said, reaching out a hand to me. "Would you do me the honor?" he asked.

I noticed he was just being playful, so I accepted his offer and let him lead me to the dance floor. Tex eyed us as we made our way. Magnus' father caught on to the glare and leaned in to whisper something to T.C. With a nod of his head, he confirmed what Edgar had wondered.

I danced twice with Magnus and once with his father. For an elderly man, he moved surprisingly well. The last dance was, and please sit down if you are not sitting already, T.C. That's right, you read correctly. Tex's father moved over to us and asked Edgar if he could kindly cut in. I had to steel my nerves and plaster on my fake face before allowing myself to be swept up in a dance. I purposefully averted my gaze.

"Ms. Ayers, I know you haven't the least desire to dance with, yet alone associate with me in the slightest."

"Now, why on earth would you think that?" I mocked sweetly.

I felt his grumble of a laugh reverberate through his chest. "Tex told me you had a knack for sarcasm," he breathed heavily, "but I did not catch you up in this dance to have it out with you."

"Then why dance with me at all?"

He stopped the dance. I looked up at him, eyebrows furrowed and anger seething at my spine. But he wasn't glaring at me or even giving me that hateful disposition he usually has when at the dinner table or commenting on my gypsy heritage.

With a serious expression, he said plainly, "To tell you how very sorry I am for all the hurt and pain I caused you."

With his next few words, my hands dropped from his, and my heart broke. I listened with tears spilling down my face as Texas Conrad the Third asked for my forgiveness.

"Please, Selena," he said softly, a hitch in his voice. Truthfully, that broke me a little. In all the time I've known this belligerent man, he has never called me by my name. "Back then," he continued after somewhat composing himself, "I was an arrogant fool who made big business and the next dollar my focus in life. It has cost me the love of my wife and son."

His big hands grabbed one of mine and grasped it. I watched his lips quiver a little as he made himself push past his pride and continue.

"Texas would never have betrayed you if it hadn't been for me. I know he made a choice and he certainly could have defied me sooner, but I was his father and a bully. All I ask is that you accept my apology, for I do mean every word, and that you try to find it in your heart to forgive my son. I know he deserves your anger, but I ask that you place that rage with me. If you are resisting forgiveness because of the hurt he caused you, then so be it. I ask you, just don't let it be because of the stupidity of this old man."

I stood there as he brought me into a hug, not moving and not hugging back. Even after he'd walked away, my mind was still whirling with what he'd said. Every word haunted me as I made my way back to the table. I noticed Texas and his mother had gone. Others rose, but I told them it wasn't necessary and shook their hands before excusing myself to my room.

Magnus thanked me for the dance, and I felt a slip of paper in my hand as he pulled away. I offered them all a final smile and headed to the elevator. It was a blessing to find it empty. My reflection peered back at me from the shiny doors. I was a mess, inside and out.

When the doors opened, I zombie-walked into my suite and immediately turned to the small table where the phone and lamp sat. I placed my bag down and slid out of my shoes while I read the small piece of paper.

I noticed your eyes often found young Texas as we danced. If you're ever not taken, please give me a call.

Magnus Van Hoffman

304-529-1817

I smirked and threw the paper in the trash. He was certainly bold. Probably explained why he and his father were so successful in their business endeavors. It wasn't until I walked beside the bed that I noticed the scent. It was the only cologne he ever wore, and it was intoxicating.

"Tex," I breathed and closed my eyes before turning to find him on the other side of the bed, leaning against the post. "I'm not surprised, but I am curious. How did you get in here?" I asked him.

He began to walk toward me. I responded by moving back. He reached into his pocket and pulled out another key before flicking it away with his fingers. The whole time, he didn't speak. He just kept his eyes on me. My back found the wall.

"I guess being the wealthy vice president of a multi-million-dollar company has its perks," I said.

He only gave a nod of agreement as he continued to move toward me.

I swallowed, "Tex…um…"

I was going to ask him not to get any closer. I had every

intention of begging him not to touch me or look at me as he was anymore because I was not strong and I couldn't take it. But I never said anything.

Before any more words could escape my mouth, his hands were in my hair and grasping my neck. His mouth was on mine, and his body pressed me into the wall.

Please, just don't be ashamed of me, or at least maybe try to have a little sympathy. This was the man to whom I had been hopelessly devoted all those years before. Yes, yes, I know I had promised myself to another, and I have no excuses. Nothing I can say will make what was happening an okay thing. It's pathetic, really. I was holding this vengeful grudge against Texas, and here I was acting no better, actually worse.

The material of the shameless burgundy dress bunched as it slid from my shoulders and down my body to the floor. A gasp of longing escaped my lips as he swept me into his arms and carried me to the bed. Our lips never left each other, and he allowed me a tear or two as he folded me into him and took from me what I wouldn't vocally give but didn't physically deny.

***

The sun warmed my face, and I awoke pleasantly. Sleeping in a high-dollar hotel means high-dollar sleep. In other words, it wasn't just the night's events that relaxed me. Alright, it was mostly the events, but this bed was super comfy as well.

I hated myself as I showered and fixed my hair to prepare for the courtroom. I noticed the flower and note on the table where I'd left my bag.

I love you.

That was all that was written on the small hotel parchment. To anyone else, it was just three little words, but I knew how much was put into each one. I didn't have time for this. I couldn't sit there and try to sort through my feelings. I had a job to finish. So I dropped the note, grabbed my favorite skirt suit, and disappeared into the bathroom.

twenty-six

TECHNICALLY, I'M AN OMITTER...NOT A LIAR

B y the end of the day on that Friday, Generations had proven their commitment to protecting the environment while still creating jobs and providing service to the nation. They had won. The story made national headlines everywhere, and since I had the exclusive, my report was being picked up by the masses. When we arrived back at Saint Caine, there was a large celebration held in the building. Everyone came. We had music, food, and lots of toasts.

I was dancing with Ryan when Tex asked to steal me for a moment. Ryan, being the gentleman he is, politely allowed him to do so. He told Tex to handle me with care, to which he replied, "That's the plan." Ryan thought he meant just the dance. I knew better.

Tex moved me around a few times, staring down at me as he did so. I finally grinned and blushed, making myself look away. It was nice to see him this way. I could tell he was feeling happy as he tilted his head and grasped my hand. And then, a split second later, he was furious. My eyes grew to saucers as his fingers snatched my ring finger and the diamond placed on it.

"Why are you still doing this?" he snarled at me.

"Doing what?" I asked, knowing precisely what he meant.

He pulled me right up against him and held my back as we swayed in place, whispering fiercely into my ear, "Why are you still pretending with him?"

"I'm not pretending, Tex," I argued.

"Oh, really," he said, looking to find Ryan at the bar talking to Mr. Harmon. "If you aren't pretending with him, then what was Dallas?"

I dropped my head a little. "That was…it was a…"

"Mistake?" he asked, stopping our swaying and staring down at me.

I jerked my head up and held his gaze. "No! I wasn't going to say that at all."

Tex's arm relaxed behind me. He unclenched his jaw, and we began to sway again. "Then you'll tell him?"

"Tell him?" I asked, shocked. "You want me to tell him?"

"I want you to tell him that you are in love with me. You've always been in love with me, and you can't marry him."

"This isn't fair, Texas. You knew before the trip that Ryan and I were together and had been for quite some time." I looked around and lowered my voice to a fierce whisper as well. "You were also very much aware that he and I were going through a tough time when you broke into my suit and…"

"Made love to you," he finished.

I stiffened this time and bit at my bottom lip. This got a sly smirk out of him. I narrowed my eyes as I said, "You are insufferable."

"No, my dear," he told me, swaying back and forth to

the music, "I'm not insufferable, just impatient. I'm in love with you, and I want you to marry *me*, not him."

Had those words actually come out of his mouth? I was stunned. I knew he wanted me back and had attributed most of that to just jealousy over Ryan, but had he seriously said he wanted to marry me? This, I could not handle. Not right now. "Can we not do this here, now?" I asked pleadingly.

Over at the bar, Mr. Harmon was joined by Patty as he was talking with Ryan. She congratulated Ryan on our engagement, and he thanked her. Mr. Harmon's cell rang, and he had to excuse himself to hear the call properly. This left the perfect invitation for the high school version of Miss Patty K. to release her claws. It was like senior year all over again.

"You sure are a trusting man," she purred at Ryan.

"It's just a dance, Patty, and I can see her perfectly from here."

Patty laughed a little too heartily, which caught Ryan's attention. "What?" he asked her. "Are you saying there's something I should know?" My reassurances about the tabloids weren't as effective as I had hoped.

He put his drink on the bar and turned to face her.

"You mean you don't already?" she asked him silkily.

He gave her a confused look and shook his head back and forth. Patty laughed again, handed him his drink, and said, "Here, doll, you're going to need it."

The music was winding down. Tex and I had started talking, believe it or not, about things other than us. I told him about dad and his fantasy sports teams, which made him laugh, and told me a story about a time when he and dad had made up a whopper of a tale to Jimmy Langley, dad's co-worker, about Tom Brady, which secured him the trade. We were both laughing together when I looked over and saw Ryan's face.

All the sound rushed from the room as I took in the scene before me. Patty leaned toward him, working her lips like crazy to tell him all that she could in the time she had. I saw Ryan's facial expressions narrow and harden. Not a minute later, he was stalking toward us. Behind him, I saw Patty give me an evil grin and wave her fingers at me as if she had just handed me a gift.

"Oh no," I breathed out.

Tex looked at me and turned in time to see Ryan step toward the both of us.

"Selena, we are leaving," Ryan demanded, and then he turned his attention to Texas. "Get your hands off of my wife," he snarled.

My eyes shifted downward, and I saw Tex's hands slowly glide up to his waist. *Please, Lord, no*, I thought.

"She's not your wife," Tex told him, glaring back into Ryan's eyes as viciously as he was staring into Tex's. "Last I checked, she was still Selena *Ayers*."

In a swift movement, Ryan snatched my hand and held the diamond up to his face. "She's as good as. In case you didn't notice, that's an engagement ring. I'll thank you for keeping your distance from now on."

"No need to thank me. I won't be doing it." Tex shot back at him, and then his jaw clenched as his eyes narrowed, and I quickly piped up and got between them.

"You're right, Ryan. It is late, and I'm ready to go," I pushed at him a little, making his feet turn as I did.

Tex took his eyes off Ryan to look down at me. "Thank you for the dance," I said hurriedly, "but we need to go. I still haven't been to my parents yet. See you around Tex."

That was enough to make Ryan turn and stalk off toward the doors. I followed him, stopping only to let Patty know what a despicable, wretched person I thought she was.

"Are you talking about me, hon?" she asked, feigning confusion. "Or yourself. Because I am pretty sure you could have told him everything I just did, long before now."

I glared at her. As much as I just wanted to pull a Cassey and sink my fist in her face, I knew she was right. This moment would have never happened if I had just told Ryan everything from the start.

Still, I thought, cocking my head, what business was it for this wench? So, in true childish fashion, I raised my voice to our surrounding audience and said, "You know, Pats, you're right. We should all let everyone know exactly what hidden things we share from our past. Since you shared mine, let me do the same for you." I turned to the crowd. "In sophomore year, Patty K. Harmon here got an S.T.D. from one of the football players of our rival school." I heard a balk of laughter and grinned wider as Patty's eyes grew into saucers. I continued quickly, seeing Tex making his way towards us. "She doesn't know that I knew about this because she went to a clinic outside of town. But," I added, smiling sweetly at Patty, "my mother's stepsister was the clerk at that clinic, and I spent that evening helping her put away files before going out to celebrate my mom's fortieth."

I gave her that little finger wave she always gave me, then rushed to the doors Ryan had just sped through. I looked behind my shoulders to see that Tex had been caught up by Mr. Van Hoffman. From where he was, that lot wouldn't have heard anything I had said, but the little group around me and Patty were laughing hysterically. She cast them all malicious looks before slinging back her hair and stomping off to find her husband.

Ryan had already pulled the car around and was

waiting for me. I opened the door and got in, trying hard to fasten my seat belt as he squealed out of the parking lot.

"Would you mind slowing down?" I asked him.

"Would you mind telling me why I had to find out from the building gossip about you and Texas Conrad?" he barked.

I touched his arm. "Ryan, please, let's just go to my place and talk about this."

"Does he know where you live?" he asked.

Closing my eyes, I reluctantly admitted, "Yes. He knows where I live."

Ryan snorted, "Then your place is out. We're going to mine."

I sat back against the seat and worked at my bottom lip. I had never seen Ryan in this state. He has always been so laid-back and fun-loving. I'd never seen him get worked up over a case he was having trouble with or plans he had been making that fell through. I watched him pityingly as he worked his jaw muscles, grinding his teeth in anger. Realizing this was going to be a long night, I rested my head against the window and scolded myself for being so stupid.

Ryan slammed the door behind me, tore his tie from his neck, and unbuttoned the top buttons of his shirt as he stomped into the living room. My heels clacked the ceramic tile as I followed.

I got in the room to find him pacing back and forth. His sleeves were now pulled up, and his hands were folded together on top of his head. I waited patiently for him to address me.

"Why, Selena?" he asked calmly, still not taking his hands from his head, "Why didn't you tell me?"

When I didn't answer right away, he dropped his hands into his pockets and looked at me. I shrugged my shoulders and shook my head. "I don't know," I said, dropping into the large, overstuffed chair by the fireplace. "I mean, I know why I didn't at first, but I don't know why I didn't at all."

"Then why didn't you at first?" he asked, sitting across from me in the other chair. He was leaning forward with his forearms resting on his legs. His face was an expression of utter disbelief as he spoke, "Can you at least answer that? Why didn't you tell me on the beach the night I asked you what you meant by it being 'such a long time'? That's what you were talking about, wasn't it? You were referring to your relationship with him."

He knew the answer to that, but I nodded my head, acknowledging that he was right anyway. "Yes," I finally said when I could bring myself to speak. "I was talking about it being such a long time since my relationship with Tex. I didn't tell you then because that would have meant having to acknowledge it completely, and I had only managed to keep myself together by continuing to push him and everything about him to the back of my mind. By not dealing with it, I've been able to live with it."

"You should have told me," he said.

I snorted mockingly, "Oh yes, I'm sure you would have found that so attractive. This girl you've been smitten with seems perfect in every way until you find out she's been screwed up by an old flame." I looked over at him and added, "No one wants that kind of baggage."

"I wish you would have trusted me. I knew at that moment you had been hurt, and pretty badly, but I promised to make sure you never felt that again. I asked your parents, but they told me it was your story to tell and to just be patient because you would trust me with it eventually." He slung his hands down and jerked up from the seat, leaning his arm against the fireplace mantle. "But you never did," he spat.

That's one way to make a girl feel like a heaping pile of cow dung.

"I'm so sorry," I said.

He slid his eyes to me, watching me for a long moment before looking away and back towards the wall. His eyes squinted as he spoke again. "You know, it's not even that you never felt like you could trust me either. That didn't keep me from loving you or wanting to marry you. What has me so upset, so completely insane with fury right now, is that you spent all this time with him."

He slammed his fist against the wall. One of the mantle candles fell and broke, making me jump. He grumbled sorry at me as he sat down again, dropping his head down and clasping his hands behind his neck. He was taking deep breaths.

"I should have told you everything about Texas," I told him. "I know that, but this was my job. Whether I told you everything or not, I still had to do my job."

His head shot up. "You could have done your job, Selena, but I would have been fully aware of what I was up against. Did you not hear him tonight?" he asked, then said in a mocking voice of Tex's, "'*Last I checked, she was still Selena Ayers*', do you not realize he wants to get you back?"

"Yes," I admitted, not taking my eyes off him.

He swallowed. "You know, as in, like he's told you, that he wants you back?"

"Yes," I said again, letting a tear slide down my cheek.

He pursed his lips and nodded his head before asking the next question. It was obvious he was trying any way to avoid asking, but it was inevitable, and he had to know.

"I guess the next question is…" he said, raising his eyes to look at me. I noticed the whites of his eyes were reddening, and my heart ached for him. "Do you want him back?"

My lips quivered as I looked hastily away. I needed to

steel my nerves before answering. Turns out it wasn't necessary as Ryan hastily spit out, "Don't answer that!" as he
rose from the seat again.

I looked up at him as he paced a couple of times.
Finally, he paused right in front of me and dropped to his
knees. He grabbed my hand and touched the diamond,
moving it back and forth on my finger.

"I'm going to say this, and then I'm going to bed. So
please just listen, and afterward," he stopped a moment to
shake his head before speaking again, "well, that will be
entirely up to you. So, that being said. If you want him
back, then I won't stand in your way. I love you, Selena. I
truly do. I will not hurt you in any way, and that includes by
trying to guilt you into staying with me when you want to
be with him." He touched my ring once more. "But I ask
you to think about this. He had you. He had everything
that he wanted, and he treated it as if it didn't matter. He
hurt you for his social status and bankroll. Selena, I will
never hurt you."

He stood there for a moment, just looking at me. I swallowed down my tears, watching him as he watched me.
Gently, he touched a strand of my hair, letting the curl slide
around his finger.

"If you go to him, Selena, I'll have to leave. There is no
way I could watch that man live my happiness. But if you
still want to marry me, if you love me and still want to
enjoy this happiness that you and I have and that we will
always have together, then I'll be waiting for you upstairs. If
you do choose me, though, I need you to put Texas Conrad
out of our lives for good, and in return, I promise I'll never
bring this up again."

He reached down and kissed me longingly on the lips
before heading up the stairs.

I sat alone downstairs for a long time. I cried, and I

fought with myself. I even picked up my phone a couple of times, considering calling Cass and Amber. Goodness, I was such a mess. I almost even called Mom. But in the end, as I rubbed my finger over my bottom lip, I thought about the past and what Ryan had said. Tex had me once, and he did treat that as though it were nothing. True, Ryan didn't know everything—like what I had just learned about Tex's dad and the business and all that—but there was truth at the heart of what he had said. Was it possible that it could happen again? What if, a couple of years down the road, there is another big business issue?

It was unlikely, I guess, and his dad really did seem apologetic, but still, wasn't having that possibility enough to scare me away from ever tempting fate that way again? It was Grandma Pearl I ended up calling. She answered before the first ring even finished.

"Selena Marie, it is time you trusted in your intuition," she admonished. "My guidance can only get you so far. You are split apart into two even halves, and there is only one choice that will get you whole again. Just remember, no matter what the outcome, your family loves you, and you will always have us."

"I love you, Nana," I told her.

They were the only words I spoke to her. I hung up the phone, walked over to the door, and turned the lock. Upstairs, Ryan was still wide awake. I slid under the sheets and snuggled up beside him. He wrapped his arm around me and held me tight. He never said a word, and neither did I.

twenty-seven

NOW WHAT?

ngaged? The word ran through Tex's head so many times that he was considering taking a hammer to his skull just to see if he could get it to stop. Even when he closed his eyes, he could see it slowly slithering beneath his lids. Engaged.

His anger and frustration were at boiling point, and there was nothing he could do other than find some way to vent it all out. So here he was in the gym of his building, standing in front of the worn-out heavy bag after pulling on some shorts, an old high school football t-shirt, and having taped and gloved his hands. There was a small *crack* as he moved his neck side to side and around to loosen up his muscles. Bouncing on his feet, he imagined the bag was Ryan James and set to work beating the crap out of it.

By the time he had punched and kicked until he was too exhausted to move another inch, he wrapped his arms around the bag and held his forehead against it, breathing ragged as he did. *Engaged*. Taking one good deep breath, he gave the bag a final half-hearted punch before turning and sluggishly scooting his way to the wooden bench in front of the wall of lockers. He plopped down, facing the still-swinging bag, and gulped a large drink of water from the bottle. My face hovered in his mind as he leaned back against the lockers and closed his eyes, waiting for his breathing to regulate and his pulse to slow.

After Dallas, he thought everything was going to just work itself out. He had made love to me and I had let him. Not only that, I had let him *knowing* that I'd said yes to marrying Ryan. That had to mean something. A nasty little imp of a thought wriggled at his consciousness, spitting in a malicious voice that perhaps she did so as a way of saying goodbye indefinitely. That what had happened in Dallas had been some type of closure for her.

No, no, he wouldn't believe that. He shot up from the bench so fast that the water bottle toppled and hit the floor. Tex groaned as the liquid pooled around his feet. Just great —one more thing to irritate him. He snatched the mop from the supply room behind the weight bench and brought it over to clean up the spill. A smile ghosted his face as he thought about how horrified his father would be if he saw his son cleaning up like one of the building employees. Tex didn't mind it though. He rather enjoyed being able to do things like this—to be able to make a mess and clean it up. That's what he was doing with his life, wasn't it? He'd turned it into one royal mess years ago, and he has slowly, project by project, stance by stance, been working to clean up all the debris left in its wake.

That was it, then. His head snapped up, and he looked at his reflection in the wall of mirrors behind the bag he'd just walloped. Over the years, he'd been able to break the generational curse of being judgmental and prejudiced in his family. He'd somehow gotten his father to go from an overbearing belligerent fool to a somewhat decent human being, and he even had these past months to work on apologizing to me and finding ways to assure me that I can trust him and that he will never hurt me again. He just had some more cleaning up to do, that was all. Ryan wasn't a wrench in his plans; he was merely an inconvenience to his time frame. A ring on a finger isn't a done deal. Isn't that the main premise of almost every romantic movie ever made? Get the girl before she says, "I do", right? Tex laughed out loud to himself while tossing a towel over his shoulder and heading to the elevator that would take him back up to his top-floor condo. It wasn't over, not by a long shot. Ryan James may have put a ring on my finger before he could, but Tex would be the man getting the "I do" when all was said and done.

Just like when he devised a plan in the past, he went to work on another. The one thing he knew he absolutely could not do was let me push him out of my life. This was going to be the hardest part because if Ryan was even half as jealous as Tex, then he was currently making sure I was promising to cut all ties immediately. Another chuckle reverberated through his lips as Tex stepped into his condo and headed for the kitchen. Another cold bottle of water, and he was headed for the shower. He'd decided to give the whole thing a couple of days to blow over, then he would call, text, or even show up at my house. He meant it when he told me he was going to do whatever it took, and until there was truly no hope left, he intended to keep his word on that.

twenty-eight
SOMETHING'S GOTTA GIVE

For almost a full month, I had dodged Tex's emails, phone calls, and even his visits to my home. I had taken to staying at Ryan's to give him peace of mind and to avoid any further confrontations. We were practically living a married couple's life already. We made breakfast, we went to work, we made dinner, and then we would either watch a movie or hang out with Pete and Amber. Sometimes even Cassey and Derek would show up.

I don't know how long I expected this to last before Texas broke. I guess I was back to doing that thing where if I avoided something, I didn't have to deal with it. You would think I would have learned that wasn't the case. But I hadn't learned it, and here it was staring me right in the face.

Cass, Amber, and I were all at the bridal shop for fittings. I had just tried on dress number four and trudged back into the fitting room. I shut the door behind me but spun around as I heard the lock snap shut. Texas was in the room, and he was mad.

"What are you doing here?" I asked him, gathering the dress against me.

He raised an eyebrow. "I've seen everything under that dress, Selena. There is no sense in playing coy."

I let the dress drop and went over to the door, shoving him out of the way. I quickly opened it, looked out to make sure the coast was clear, and came back in, shutting and locking the door once more. I faced him. This room was a nice size, but with him in it, the walls and ceiling seemed smaller. I let my eyes scan the room, mentally ticking off things I saw to help calm me down before I addressed the menace causing my anxiety. A full-sized three-way mirror in front of a standing podium to my left. A rack of various wedding dresses hung on a rolling bar straight across from me, and to my right was a small sitting table with champagne flutes and ice-chilling expensive champagne in the middle of two very comfortable chairs. The carpet, room, and even the chairs and tablecloth were all in a soft lavender. Fairy lights were strung up around the room and twirled down with soft green ivy in every corner. I closed my eyes, breathed deeply, and opened them to stare right at Tex.

"You can't do this, Tex," I told him, "you can't just show up whenever you feel like it."

"It seems that I can, as I have done it in the past and will continue to do so as long as you keep refusing my calls and ignoring me."

"Did it occur to you that I don't want to talk to you?"

"No," he answered nonchalantly, "what did occur to me is that your boyfriend threw a fit and demanded you break all contact with me, and since we both know how you avoid conflict at all costs, you were more than willing to comply as long as it meant him not being upset anymore."

"That is…" I growled, shoving another dress over my

lingerie, "the most ridiculous thing I've ever heard." I reached around to try and zip the dress. Tex moved my arms out the way and pulled the zipper up for me.

"This dress is hideous, by the way," he told me in a matter-of-fact tone.

I gave him a dirty look before turning to the mirror. After a little consideration, I reached back to unzip it instead.

"I told you," he balked.

I gave up. I threw my hands up in the air, stomped over to the dressing chair, and crashed my body down into it.

"I can't do this," I complained.

He rolled his eyes and said, "Just come here, and I'll unzip it."

"No," I laughed, and then I cried, "this! I can't do this." I told him, flinging my hand back and forth between us.

"And I can't let you go," he told me, resting his body against the wall in front of me.

We stared at each other. Then Tex moved off of the wall and walked over to me. He held out his hands, and I took them with my own. Pulling back, he raised me to my feet. He was so gorgeous. He had always been. I pouted my lip out, and he laughed under his breath.

"I'm not going to give up, Selena," he whispered to me, cupping my head in his hands. He continued to use his thumbs to caress my jawline as he looked into my eyes. I saw his lids close as he brought our mouths together. I started to close my eyes as well, to just give in, as I had in the hotel suite all those weeks ago, but I didn't. It took everything in me, but I managed to reach up, cup his hand in my own, and slide back away from him. Since a sob of tears was threatening to choke me up completely, I could only whisper as I said, "I can't, Tex. Not anymore, okay?"

Texas was a gentleman, as always. He released my arms

and slowly backed away from me. "Alright, Selena," he said, "I will respect your wishes to not try anything physical with you while you are intent on marrying this man that you and I both know you do not truly love. Not like you love me." When I opened my mouth to argue, he held up his hand, reaching the other hand back to open the dressing room door. "Don't bother trying to deny it. I know you better than anyone else. So I'll keep my distance when it comes to that, but I will not let this go. I will not drop this. The way I see it, I have precious little time left in which to convince you of the horrible mistake you will be making in following through with this. I will not quit until it truly is too late."

"Wonderful," I quipped, "so glad I get to star in one of those cheesy romantic comedies where the preacher asks for objections and my ex-boyfriend is going to break his neck to make sure he is recognized as someone who vehemently disagrees."

That delicious smirk lit on Tex's face as he turned his head back over his shoulder to tell me as he walked away, "Hopefully it won't come to that," he winked at me, "I'll see you around, beautiful."

And so it went for the next few months. Tex would show up out of nowhere in places I never would have dreamed to see him. On more than one occasion, he was waiting for me in my home when he somehow knew that Ryan was not going to be with me that night.

The majority of the time, we ranted and raved at one another. He was constantly telling me to call this stupid wedding off and come back to him, and I was always telling him I couldn't do that and that Ryan deserved better. We would fuss well into the night, and then there would be flowers or some other gift waiting for me the next day.

But then there were the other times when I was too

exhausted to fight and Tex wouldn't berate me about Ryan and our *"mistake of a wedding"* or anything else that was certain to cause another row. We would just talk about our lives over the years and how things are going now with our careers. I even caught him up on all the drama between Cassey and Derek. Those times were nice. Even though I am marrying Ryan, I can't help thinking about how nice it would be to at least have my friend Tex back in my life. We were madly in love back then, but the best part of it all was that he was another best friend, and after spending so much time together these past months, I've been reminded how much I missed that part of him. After those times, I would find myself wondering if I had that same friendship with Ryan. I was attracted to him, and he made me happy enough. I had a lot of fun with him, but as a best friend, well, that was not quite there yet, I guess.

In no time at all it was August. Texas had demanded I call it off for the millionth time, and I *again* told him I just couldn't. Instead of a super fun bachelorette party that had been meticulously planned by Amber which was to take place in the city where we would be entertained by attractive men in very skimpy underwear dancing for use, the three of us tucked our legs up on the velvet red sofa of the V.I.P. booth, where I unloaded everything I had kept to myself onto Cassey and Amber. The others got to enjoy the entertainment, though, so it wasn't a total waste. Amid a cat call and a shameful whistle, the three of us picked apart my relationships and analyzed them with the precision of a molecular biologist. I had expected them to blow up at me, especially Cass. From her, I had even anticipated some violence. But all they did was wrap their arms around me and tell me that no matter what, they would be there.

twenty-nine

YES, DEFINITELY WEDDING BELLS

How did we get here so fast? I'm certain you are reading back again, trying to see if you missed something along the way or if there was a tidbit about Ryan you must have overlooked. You're right in knowing there had to be more. But when it came to Ryan, everything just sailed along. He was content with putting faith in the choice I made that night at his place. Since there was no longer a need for me to spend time with Generations Steel and since I had made quite a name for myself, I was able to do the majority of my work from home.

I have written several pieces for major news networks. Ryan had won his last three cases, and with all the wedding hustle and bustle, he was true to his word and never brought it up again. I plastered on my "everything is just perfect" face and allowed us both to live by the old saying that *"ignorance is bliss"*.

The big day had finally come, and I was alone in a room of the sanctuary, standing by a glass-stained window barely cracked open enough to see the beautiful green of the grass and trees just outside. I looked up at the sky and started to smile until I saw a small grayish cloud, which seemed kind of ominous and looming. I shrugged to myself. It made sense, I guess. All the happiness comes with a little bit of hesitation. My thoughts and I were trying to get along when I heard Tex's voice come from my right.

"Come with me," he said, "just get up, leave the dress and all this nonsense, and come with me. I'll fly us anywhere you want to go. We can stay gone as long as you like until this whole thing blows over."

I didn't turn around. I hadn't even jumped when he spoke, a part of me knowing that there was no way this day was going to happen without him giving all that he had to stop it. I sighed, my eyes dropping with hurt and worry. "Then what?" I asked him.

"What do you mean?"

"I mean, then what after?" I said, finally turning around to face him. He was wearing nice slacks and a tight-fit button-up navy shirt with a navy and silver-striped tie. Just looking at him took my breath away, he will always be so devastatingly handsome. I met his eyes with my own. "What will happen after it is all settled down? What if your business gets into jeopardy again, or your father decides perhaps you can do better than some small, talented gypsy? What then?"

"Believe me, it is never going to happen. I will *not* make the same mistake twice," he told me.

"Should I?" I asked him. He knew I was asking if I should make the same mistake twice, not whether or not I should believe him. I was so defeated that all I could do was continue to stare into his eyes.

The question lingered in the air. I watched his jaw muscles clench and unclench. He pinched his nose between his thumb and finger before coming over to me and wrapping me up in a hug. He held onto the back of my head and kissed the side of my face. I didn't protest. I knew these ministrations were ones of just caring and kindness, not about demanding sexual reciprocation.

"You're right," he said softly, "I've been so determined to prove to you that I wouldn't make that same mistake. I was so relentless in trying to prove it that I never considered you would be making that same promise to yourself, and you would have every right to."

He kissed my face again and hugged me tightly, never letting his lips move from my ear.

"I know, Selena, without a shadow of a doubt, that if you came back to me, I would never, ever hurt you again. I know that I would do everything to make sure you were happy and loved, and that you never wanted for a thing in this life. I know this, but the fact is, unless you know it as well, you will always be wondering and never be happy."

He pulled me back from him. With a small, sad smile on his lips, he used the pad of his thumb to wipe the tear from my face. "I love you so much that I am willing to make any sacrifice necessary for you to be truly happy. So if that means I have to leave here now and let you go, then that's what I'll do. Not because I want to. Lord knows it is the last thing I want. But if it is what is best for you and your future, then I will love you from afar only."

My face tilted upward as he drew his lips down to mine. Each motion of his lips brought a wave of pain through my heart. This was the goodbye we never got to all those years ago. Perhaps this would have been the end of our prom night had I not taken off before it could play out. I could give him this. I can give him a kiss goodbye. A last kiss for the man I fell so deeply in love with that the idea of living without him almost pulled me apart. Too soon he was sliding out of my grasp, and just moments after that, he was gone.

Amber knocked on the door. It had been over two hours since Texas had left. I was sitting in the office chair before the desk, where the preacher would no doubt sit and fuss over what Sunday's sermon would be about. I was fully dressed, flowered up, and, by the looks of it, all ready to go.

"Thirty minutes, hon," Amber said, smiling at me. Cassey burst in beside her, holding out her phone for a last *"single selfie"* as she called it.

They both stopped in their tracks and looked at me. Their expressions slowly filled with mischievous glee. I think I mentioned I had the best BFFs in the world already, right?

thirty

WHAT DID YOU EXPECT?

Tex sat in his old room at the estate, staring into the fireplace. When he'd left the church, he intended to go home but he found himself back here. Back where he'd lost me. He had poured himself a drink, which he didn't normally do, but tonight seemed like a good time to make an exception. He had lost everything. Anyone around him now would no doubt say, *"Suck it up, buttercup, you're a multi-millionaire for goodness sake. Shouldn't we all have it so hard?"* But to Tex, all the money in the world was not worth losing what he had. He stood up and walked over to the mantle, his hand reaching out as he did. My picture was framed at the end, next to our homecoming dance snapshot. It was a picture in which I was wearing a black two-piece bikini and sunglasses. I was looking at the camera and sticking out my tongue. Tex smirked, running his thumb over my face.

His eyes misted over a little as he reminisced about that day all those years ago. What a fool he had been. What a stupid, selfish, arrogant brat to believe he could just make everyone happy and get everything he wanted without considering what that meant to the people he would be hurting. Honestly! It truly made him sick to think about how sure of his good looks and wealth he was that he could be denied nothing if he really wanted it. That kind of thinking was the only personality flaw he could say he had inherited from his father. He'd thankfully cut that nonsense from his life since. The sound of tapping against the large windows started to increase in intensity. It had started raining a little over an hour ago. Texas thought this was fitting as it coincided with the breaking of his heart. "Even the sky is sobbing," he said out loud to no one. When my picture refused to speak to him, he placed it back on the mantle and turned to head down the stairs.

The sky chose that moment to rumble, and a sizzling snap lit up the sky and room below. A flash of white from the corner of his eye shocked him, and he quickly whipped his head around just as a second flash lit everything once more. In a fluid motion, he streaked to the door, flinging it open as he dashed outside into the downpour. He was immediately soaked, and his chest was rising and falling rapidly, trying to catch his breath from the run. A smirk cocked the side of his face as he took me in. My hair was dripping and sodden around my face. My make-up had run to my neck. A part of my wedding dress had torn on the way up the stairs, and I was sobbing uncontrollably.

Tex's smile slowly grew into a boisterous grin, his eyes twinkling with delight. At that moment, I was the most beautiful thing he had ever seen.

epilogue

ALL'S WELL THAT ENDS WELL!

Alright, now calm down. Before you decide to hate me and my choices, please hear the rest of our little tale.

When it comes to Ryan, you don't need to be so upset. Remember when he told me that he wanted me to be happy, even if that meant my happiness wasn't with him? Well, he meant what he said. The man is honestly one of the best people I have ever met, and the woman who ends up with him is going to be a very lucky lady indeed. His future panned out really well. Although he did leave Saint Caine as he said he would have to, he used his recommendations from Harmon and Associates to gain a partnership at a very prestigious firm in upstate New York. We have kept in touch over the past few years, and as I predicted, he found love again. He celebrated his engagement to an equally successful lawyer in his new firm just a couple of weeks ago.

As for me and Texas, you may be wondering if he finally did right by me as he said he would, or did we befall another heartbreaker, and wouldn't that just serve me right?

I'll just leave you with this. It's Christmas day in the

Conrad household as our entire family sits comfortably in the family den at the estate. I am typing my last few lines as I look around the room. Tex's mother, Amelia, is chatting with my mother beside the Christmas tree. They are giggling uncontrollably. About what, I have no idea, but I suspect it has something to do with a complaint either woman has against their husband. T.C., who is holding a bear wearing a Cowboy's uniform, is sitting on the couch beside my father. He too is holding a stuffed animal, and his animal is wearing a Texans jersey. Both parents are wiggling their perspective toys in the face of my husband, Texas. He is laughing and bouncing his knee to the sheer glee of our son, Texas Conrad the Fifth...

Something or other...

THANK YOU FOR READING

Did you enjoy this book?

We invite you to leave a review at your favorite book site, such as Goodreads, Amazon, Barnes & Noble, etc.

DID YOU KNOW THAT LEAVING A REVIEW...

- Helps other readers find books they may enjoy.
- Gives you a chance to let your voice be heard.
- Gives authors recognition for their hard work.
- Doesn't have to be long. A sentence or two about why you liked the book will do.

about the author

Samantha D. Long was born and raised in Ohio, but currently hangs her hat in Grayson, Kentucky. She spends her days teaching, being a wife and mother, and writing awesome stories of course! She received a Bachelor' degree in The Science of Education for Mathematics and Language Arts from Ohio University, which mostly taught her how to use the personalities, quirks, and odious aura of demanding professors as foundations for some of her characters. When not reading or writing, she enjoys playing video games and spending way too much time watching people fall down on TikTok.

instagram.com/authorteacher77

facebook.com/samanthalong1977

tiktok.com/@wndrwmn77

x.com/samanthalong77